D0305702

Constable on Trial

By the same author

Murder at Maddleskirk Abbey
A Full Churchyard
Confession at Maddleskirk Abbey

THE CONSTABLE SERIES

Constable on the Hill
Constable on the Prowl
Constable Around the Village
Constable Across the Moors
Constable in the Dale
Constable by the Sea
Constable Along the Lane
Constable Through the Meadow
Constable in Disguise
Constable Among the Heather
Constable by the Stream
Constable Around the Green
Constable Beneath the Trees
Constable in Control
Constable in the Shrubbery
Constable Versus Greengrass
Constable About the Parish
Constable at the Gate
Constable at the Dam
Constable Over the Stile
Constable Under the Gooseberry Bush
Constable in the Farmyard
Constable Around the Houses
Constable Along the Highway
Constable Over the Bridge
Constable Goes to Market
Constable Along the River-bank
Constable Around the Park
Constable in the Wilderness
Constable Along the Trail
Constable on the Coast
Constable on View
Constable Beats the Bounds
Constable in the Country
Constable Over the Hill
Constable at the Fair

CONSTABLE AT THE DOUBLE
Comprising:
Constable Around the Village
Constable Across the Moors

HEARTBEAT OMNIBUS
Comprising:
Constable on the Hill
Constable on the Prowl
Constable in the Dale

HEARTBEAT OMNIBUS VOLUME II
Comprising:
Constable Along the Lane
Constable Through the Meadow

Constable on Trial

NICHOLAS RHEA

ROBERT HALE · LONDON

First published in Great Britain 2015

ISBN 978-0-7198-1814-1

Robert Hale Limited
Clerkenwell House
Clerkenwell Green
London EC1R 0HT

www.halebooks.com

2 4 6 8 10 9 7 5 3 1

Typeset in Palatino
Printed and bound in Great Britain by
CPI Antony Rowe, Chippenham and Eastbourne

CHAPTER 1

Superintendent Askey was marching towards me as I stood near the Pier Road telephone kiosk. He had a look of fierce determination on his face and I wondered if I was due for one of his critical lectures. I tried to recall what I may have done to warrant this rather unusual visit.

'I'm glad I caught you, Rhea.'

'Good evening, sir.' I saluted even though he was in civilian clothes and clutching a dog lead, at the end of which was his grey curly-haired poodle. It was always sensible to acknowledge rank even when they were off duty; after all, this man was in charge of Strensford Division. My most senior boss, in other words. I had earlier learned his dog's name was Whisky. I considered it useful to have that kind of local knowledge at my fingertips, especially when it seemed I was about to be on the defensive.

'Hello, Whisky.' I spoke gently and patted the little animal, pleased that it wagged its tail and didn't attempt to bite off my fingers.

'Not a bad evening, Rhea. You'll be off duty soon?'

I made a show of looking at my watch. It was half past nine and, as it was June, there was still some daylight left. Soon the sky would darken, and the town's street lights would burst into life. And there would be noise from the pubs and clubs as heavily fuelled merrymakers tried to find their way home, usually to the sound of car horns and buses trying to clear a route between them.

'Another half hour, sir, provided nothing serious happens. It's been a quiet shift so far.'

'"What is this life if, full of care, we have no time to stand and stare." You'll know that poet, Rhea?' Superintendent Askey, who we referred to as Arthur behind his back, was fond of quoting Shakespeare. And others.

'Shakespeare, sir?' I made a brave attempt at an answer.

'No, Rhea. William Henry Davies. Now, there is just time for me to break my news. Sergeant Blaketon said you'd be making your point here. He asked me to confirm there are no messages for you. It's all quiet in town tonight, so far at any rate. We can all rest safe in our beds, as the poet said. Now, this is what I want to ask – how does the thought of detective work appeal to you?'

His proposal caught me by surprise and it was a moment or two before I answered. 'Yes, sir, of course I'd be interested. I've always wanted to be a detective; that was one reason for joining the force.'

'We are men of the world, Rhea, and know that a good uniform must work its way with the women, sooner or later. That's Dickens, Rhea, as I'm sure you know. So are you courting?'

'I have a steady girlfriend, sir …'

'I mention that because working with CID requires dedication and, on some occasions, very long hours. You do not work eight-hour shifts as you do on uniform duties but your senior officers will make sure you get time off where possible. The Detective Allowance caters for those extra unrecorded hours and the expense of the civilian clothes you will be wearing on duty. So if you are courting, would this role create domestic problems?'

'No, sir,' I said as convincingly as possible. 'One's duty must come first! I know my girlfriend will understand.'

'"Not once or twice in our rough island-story, the path of duty was the way to glory." Not Shakespeare, Rhea, as I am sure you know.'

'Really, sir!'

'Tennyson, as a matter of fact. Now, I will set the necessary wheels in motion but it will take a week or two before you're transferred. Changes are afoot, Rhea; the force is very seriously considering ways of modernizing the service. After all, it is more than ten years since the end of World War II; many households now have telephones and the police will soon have portable radios. New ideas and procedures will be necessary if we are to embrace those changes; we must not resist but we must adapt. In any case, the station bike is almost worn out and I doubt it will ever be replaced. Maybe an extra car for the station is too much to hope for! Anyway, my own feeling is that Strensford CID could benefit from a young detective with innovative ideas that will help to update the service at local level. You'd be on trial with our local CID for an initial period of six months. How does that sound?'

'Reforms are all right so long as they don't change anything. I think that was Mickey Mouse, sir.'

'There's many a true word spoken in jest, Rhea. Well, I must leave you to cogitate upon your future but with a record of CID work on your personal file, your career would be assured. Promotion would surely follow provided you pass the necessary exams, of course – and keep out of trouble.'

'Thank you, sir, I'll do my best and I appreciate your confidence in me.'

'You've earned it, Rhea. After all, recognizing a stolen coat two years after the theft had occurred is a remarkable feat of observation and detection. And the fact you achieved it when just out of your probationary period is quite astonishing.'

'It was nothing, sir …' I began.

'Nonsense! It had all the hallmarks of first-class police work. Such an acute sense of observation and an aptitude for crime detection must be properly harnessed, hence your recommendation for a trial period as an aide to CID. You will be known as Detective Constable Rhea once your appointment is confirmed. You will be notified when the vacancy arises – a couple of weeks or so from today. I will keep you informed. Now I bid you goodnight. Come along, Whisky.'

I watched him walk along the harbourside and thought he looked like a black-winged stilt, a rare wader bird whose enormously long legs are twice the length of those of other species. The stilt has a small body on top and yet it copes without falling over. Superintendent Askey was like that – his uniform had to be especially tailored to cater for this tiny body on top of two incredibly long legs. I wondered how he kept his balance with a pint or two of beer inside him. And I wondered if he had ever ridden a penny-farthing.

He was called Arthur after the famous comedian but he had another nickname: Hivpo. That came about due to his habit of quoting Shakespeare, one of his favourite lines being 'So shaken as we are, so wan with care', which is the first line of *Henry IV, Part One*. HIVPO in other words.

As I watched him and Whisky disappear into the oncoming darkness of the peaceful streets, I wondered why my detection and recovery of a stolen raincoat should have been so memorable to my superiors. Then I left my point at the kiosk to wend my way back to the police station to knock off duty prompt at 10 p.m., all the time going over the sequence of rather remarkable events involving that coat.

First, though, an explanation of the system of patrolling around those 'points'.

At that time – the late 1950s – there were no personal radios or mobile telephones, so the only way to contact a police officer while he or she was patrolling in town was to ring on the public telephone at a prearranged visit to a kiosk. For that purpose, the local police had divided Strensford into beats: there were six. Each involved a predetermined route around the telephone kiosks in a particular part of town. The patrolling constable had to visit each of the listed kiosks at stated times and remain there for five minutes before that time and five minutes afterwards. This was known as 'making a point' and there was half an hour between each point. The purpose was to enable the office to contact any constable either by phone or even through a personal visit – as Arthur Askey had done.

Those 'points' were more formally known by the longer and more important name of 'conference points'. The system meant that all parts of the town were visited by police foot patrols arranged in the office before the officers went out on patrol. In addition to their availability, their visible uniformed presence provided a sense of security to the people. It seemed as if dozens of bobbies were around, a splendid deterrent against criminality. One old lady told me that seeing police officers patrolling the streets was as reassuring as any insurance policy.

If you think that such carefully pre-planned patrols meant that a police officer arrived at the kiosks at the same time each day, thus alerting villains to his or her movements and whereabouts, then that was not the case. Each day, the time of the 'points' was staggered by up to thirty minutes earlier than scheduled or a like time *after* the scheduled point. It meant that an officer might arrive, say, at the kiosk standing outside the GPO at ten o'clock one day but the next day his arrival might be twenty minutes earlier or fifteen minutes later – or whatever time was decided by the office.

Those deviations were predetermined and logged, and they were displayed on a clock-like device in the police station. Not surprisingly, it was known as 'the clock' and if the clock's solitary pointer was on ten past, then our points for that day were all ten minutes after the normal times. Sounds complicated? It wasn't, once you knew how it functioned – and it did work. Detectives, of course, were supposed to be invisible and so they did not operate that system. They went out on inquiries while the rest of us went out on patrol.

Now, back to the stolen coat drama which, it seemed, had opened new opportunities in my fledgling career. This is what really happened.

In the final weeks of my two years' National Service in the RAF, and due to the fact I needed some smart civilian clothes upon being demobbed so that I could take my girlfriend dancing and enjoy outings to interesting places, I decided to buy a fashionable raincoat. I found a new one in a gentleman's shop: it fitted me perfectly, it was beautifully tailored and, by chance, it was a pale version of the RAF blue and had a smart silver-coloured lining. It was rather expensive but very handsome and I liked the highly distinctive colour. It cost the huge sum of eight guineas, or in modern money £8.40, but I couldn't resist it.

Shortly before my demobilization, I took my girlfriend, Mary, to a dance in the local village hall at Bridgeholme near our respective parents' homes. It was my new coat's first formal outing and I was pleased Mary liked it. At the village hall, I hung it in the gents' cloakroom – there was nothing to pay, no tickets issued and no attendant. Quite simply, I hung it on a hook and went into the hall to enjoy the dancing.

That's how things were in rural Yorkshire at that time. When I left the dance and went to collect my coat, it was missing. Its peg was empty, so I waited until everyone had left, hoping that whoever had removed it would have realized his error and returned it. He didn't. There was one coat left – it was a filthy brown one, worn, tattered and stained, and also far too small for me. I had to accept the awful truth that my brand new raincoat had been stolen.

I went outside to report the crime to the constable on duty. He was the local bobby from my home village a couple of miles away, and he knew me well, both as a schoolboy, then as a police cadet and, at that time, an RAF National Serviceman. He took down details but said it was unlikely my coat would be recovered. He suggested I take the dirty old brown one home, which I did; I hung it in Dad's garage to moulder. A few weeks later, I was demobbed from the RAF and returned home as a civilian, whereupon I rejoined the North Riding Constabulary. After my thirteen weeks' training at a police training centre, I was posted to Strensford. I would be on probation for two years to determine my suitability as a constable and for most of that time I would patrol the town while accompanied by a senior constable, who would be my guide and friend. His name was Joe.

Towards the end of my probationary period, a friend asked if I would exchange shifts with him. He wanted me to undertake his night shift – 10 p.m. until 6 a.m. – on New Year's Eve. I agreed; Mary was also agreeable. His shift, however, was known as 'office nights' – in other words, he would not be patrolling the streets but would spend his duty time in the office with a roaring coal fire and ample coffee-brewing facilities, not to mention a glass of champagne at midnight if Sergeant Blaketon, our shift sergeant, was agreeable. Happily, he was!

It was a quiet night with lots of celebrations in town but no complaints of trouble or excessive noise. Then, shortly after 1 a.m., the office phone rang. At that time, some of the patrolling officers were in the muster room, having their mid-shift break.

'Strensford Police, PC Rhea speaking,' I answered.

'Stan from the ambulance station, Nick. We've had a call-out to the summit of Four Mile Hill; it's snowing up there and the road is treacherous. A car has spun off the road and overturned on the moor. No other vehicle or person is involved. Our unit has arrived and the driver is wandering about dazed but he seemed uninjured so we thought we should bring him into town in case he needs hospital treatment. If not, we'll bring him to the police station for you to deal with. We got the report from a passing motorist but the car isn't driveable and there's no shelter up there.'

'Right, we'll see to him,' I replied. 'We can arrange a breakdown truck in the morning. He can always sleep in one of our cells if necessary.'

It would be about twenty minutes later when I noticed the lights of the ambulance easing into the parking area near the police station and soon I heard the front door open and the sounds of two men walking along the passage towards the inquiry counter.

When I went out to meet them, I immediately noticed the man accompanying the ambulance driver was wearing my stolen raincoat! The colour was so distinctive that I could not mistake it and, besides, it was too large for the wearer. And worse still – I knew him! He'd once had a crush on my sister. I shall call him Bob; he was an itinerant trader or scrap metal dealer as some would have described him, and unerringly dishonest. Dishonesty ran through his family's veins.

Thinking quickly, I decided not to mention my suspicions just yet and offered the visitors a cup of tea and some cake we'd brought for our New Year celebrations, bringing the pair into the office to get warm near the fire. I wanted Bob to relax and not leave the police station while I decided what to do about the coat.

As I was still a probationary constable, and as Joe, my tutor, was in the next room having his mid-shift refreshment break, I decided to seek his advice. Sergeant Blaketon was somewhere in town, visiting one of the patrolling officers. What concerned me was whether it was proper for me to arrest a suspect for stealing my own coat. I wasn't sure. Plus the thief could claim that thousands of coats had been made in that colour and to that design – if he claimed he was the rightful owner, I would have difficulty proving otherwise. I made an excuse to leave Bob and the ambulance driver for a second or two as I went to the toilet but in fact hurried to the muster room to find Joe.

'Sorry to interrupt your meal break, Joe, but there's a man in the inquiry office and he's wearing a coat of mine. It was stolen two years ago.'

'You're joking!'

'No, I'm not,' and I explained.

He listened and frowned. 'You'll have to do better than that, Nick. If I go and accuse him of stealing your coat, he'll deny it, especially as it was two years ago. He'll say he bought it. How can you prove it belongs to you? That's the big question.'

'It's too big for him, he's a small man …'

'Still not good enough. If I'm going to accuse him of stealing your coat or even arrest him, I need to be sure that it really is yours. And you haven't convinced me. That means you'll not convince others, especially in a court of law.'

There was a long pause as I struggled to convince Joe, but he was right. I had no proof. Not a scrap of evidence … and then I remembered something.

'There is something, Joe. When I bought the coat, I was in the RAF and I sewed a name-tape into it: it bore my National Service number.'

'Where did you sew it?'

'Under the wrist flap on the left sleeve,' I told him. 'If you turned back the flap, my tape and number were on the inside.'

'And what was your service number?'

I told him and he wrote it down. 'Right, we need to talk to him. You'd better come with me.'

When Joe accused Bob of stealing the coat he was still wearing, not at that stage saying it belonged to me, he denied it strenuously, saying he'd bought it a few years ago but couldn't recall from which shop.

Then Joe unleashed his thunderbolt. 'Bob, you've made a very stupid mistake. This coat belongs to PC Rhea, the constable standing here, and you stole it from a dance hall cloakroom at Bridgeholme two years ago.'

Bob looked at me, the guilt clear in his eyes, and so I quietly said, 'It's my coat, Bob.'

'No, it's not, I swear it.'

'Turn back the wrist flap on the left sleeve,' said Joe.

Bob did as requested – and there was no linen strip bearing my RAF service number. It had been removed.

'There's some strands of cotton left where you cut it out.' I pointed to the strands he'd not cut free. 'And the needle holes ...'

At that point, Bob admitted the theft and when he later appeared in court, he pleaded guilty and was fined £10. He was also put on probation for two years. A few days after the court case, two cardboard cartons containing previously stolen motorcycling outfits were returned to a farmer's garden in our village. The farmer was my girlfriend's cousin but we never knew whether Bob had returned them or whether the thieves had read about the case in the local paper and got frightened.

The twist in the tale was that Bob was not obliged to report the accident to the police. By chance, he was taken there by ambulance and even so could have declined their offer of a lift. No one was injured and no other vehicle was involved. For me, it was a Happy New Year even if my coat was unwearable due to its rough treatment over its two-year absence. When a note of the case appeared in my police service personal file, it never recorded that the coat had been stolen from me.

Then when the crime reports were searched, there was no record of the theft. I was asked several times if I had reported it and I confirmed that I had. I gave the name of the officer to whom I had made my report – the local bobby from my home village – but after a long search of official records, he admitted he had listed it as lost property, not stolen! He did so because it would avoid the problem of having an unsolved theft on his rural beat and also remove the requirement to submit a crime report. He got an almighty rocket from the chief constable.

Thereafter, official accounts of the case made it appear that I had recognized and recovered a raincoat stolen from a dance hall two years earlier, which, I suppose, was true. None of the reports recorded that the coat was my own property.

Whenever I appeared before promotion boards in the years following, I was quizzed about the case, and always explained I had identified the coat because it had belonged to me. But the official records were never amended. Successive senior officers thought I had solved an amazing case by recognizing something that had been stolen two years earlier.

Having my coat stolen turned out to be a very good career move!

CHAPTER 2

'WELCOME TO THE nerve centre of this hallowed establishment, Nick,' said a smiling Detective Sergeant Tom Latimer, a large, rotund and genial man with a mop of very dark hair, always neatly groomed. I was reporting to his office for my first day's duty as a detective. 'This is where the real work gets done!' he added. 'Sit down, make yourself at home. We need to have a chat.'

I settled on a chair at the side of his desk. My previous work in this police station had made me familiar with the layout of the CID offices and I knew all the detectives – Ds as they called themselves. They occupied the entire upper floor, which contained an office for Detective Inspector Baldwin, another for Detective Sergeant Latimer and a large one shared by the four detective constables. There were toilet facilities in a former bathroom constructed more than a century earlier, and a small dressing room that had been designed and furnished as the interview room.

After a brief introductory chat, DS Latimer showed me around, explaining the whereabouts of files and confidential information I should know about. The CID's own filing system and indexed records were explained to me, these being quite separate from the police station's main recording systems. I was also shown a locked safe that contained security-sensitive files, many relating to local Nazi sympathizers from World War II.

DS Latimer then introduced me to my new colleagues. I had met them all in the normal course of my uniform duties but it felt somehow different when I became part of their world, however temporarily. My first impressions were that the CID regime was more relaxed than the uniform branch but nonetheless efficient. The staff looked happy and everything in and around the offices looked neat and tidy. I looked forward to my attachment.

DS Latimer then explained that I would share the big office with its large central table, my new colleagues being DCs Peter Salt, known as Rocky, Paul Campbell, a dour Scotsman who collected coins (and was known as a detective coinstable), Sherlock Watson, whose father had been a fan of Sherlock Holmes, and Shirley Robinson, a neat brunette whose main duties were concerned with female offenders in addition to crimes against women and children.

DS Latimer then spent some time explaining the record-keeping system. The files contained details of ongoing crime inquiries, investigations and observations as well as outstanding cases. There was also a 'dead' section of successfully completed investigations and another with cases awaiting court hearings at either magistrates' courts, quarter sessions or the assizes. Latimer reminded me that the court system was undergoing a review which was forecast to lead to the end of the quarter sessions and assizes court, both to be replaced by a single Crown Court in the foreseeable future. Crown Courts were already operating in Liverpool and Manchester where they had been introduced in 1956 as prototypes for a wider change. The death penalty for murder was also currently under review – the world of crimes and policing was ever-changing!

Some unsolved major crimes dated back several years and

their records were always open and reviewed when time and circumstances permitted. There were also lists of people who were valuable contacts in police forces throughout Britain, as well as others working in industries who might prove useful to us when making sensitive inquiries – they ranged from surgeons at Strensford Cottage Hospital to leaders of local communities and business bosses. Not to be overlooked were local informants, some of whom earned useful but secret cash payments for the information they provided to the police and security services, always in the strictest confidence.

When those preliminaries were over, I was offered a mug of coffee to sustain me during those first nervous moments as I struggled to remember everything I had been told. DS Latimer returned to his office and asked me to join him there, when he would outline my forthcoming duties. I settled once more on the chair beside his desk.

'When I did my aide attachment, Nick – a long time ago, I might add – I spent all my days filing stacks of correspondence. I think I managed to lose most of it! The old sergeant claimed it was the best way of finding out what went on in a CID office; I spent very little time out in the town hunting criminals but you'll be pleased to hear that spending all your time filing is not going to happen to you. You need to get out and about among the townspeople, getting to know the territory especially from a would-be criminal's point of view. And making acquaintance with people who will point you in the right direction – informants, I mean. We can't function without them; they are our eyes and ears.'

'Thanks,' I said with some relief. 'I'm not sure I can think like a criminal but it's the actual inquiry side of things that I find fascinating. I've always looked forward to detective work and can't wait to make my first arrest as a detective!'

'That's the spirit! I want you to actively help with our work, joining my Ds on their call-outs and inquiries whilst making your presence and local knowledge felt. The fact you recognized a stolen raincoat two years after the crime shows you have a remarkable detective acumen; we should all benefit from that.'

'It was nothing special, Sarge …' I began to attempt yet another explanation.

'You're too modest, Nick. If you're going to be successful and win promotion in this job, you've got to create an impact and make a lasting impression, so what I propose is this …' He passed a thick file of papers to me.

I placed them on the desk in front of me, unopened. 'These are crime reports covering the last twelve months. These are all undetected crimes committed in Strensford with a few from the surrounding rural area, but all within our division.'

'There's quite a pile,' I noted.

'Dead-enders mainly with little hope of being detected but I want you to find a quiet corner and go through them to see whether that observant mind of yours can throw any light on one or two. You might find our general office quiet enough when all the Ds have gone into town on their inquiries. Ask if you need anything – I've put a pad of lined notepaper in that file, which is probably why it feels so heavy. It's for your use. Ask if you want anything and don't be afraid to quiz your pals in the uniform branch to see if they can recollect any of these cases. They might have learned something new without realizing its importance. If you discover crimes you think have not been dealt with, or perhaps a witness's statement that doesn't ring true, go out and make your own inquiries to get the matters sorted. And don't forget to have your warrant card handy; you'll get loads of people asking you to prove your identity once you start asking questions. All I ask is that you let me know what you're doing and don't be afraid to ask for help if you find yourself out of your depth.'

'Thanks, Sarge.'

And so I began my fledgling new career as a D; in my case a somewhat unsure detective. I was just twenty-two years old.

The first file I examined was the most recent. There had been a series of housebreakings in town, all apparently committed by one person because in every case the same method of entry had been used. Spanning a period of about two years, they had been committed in an area of Strensford known as Birkbeck Park.

My immediate reaction was that this was peculiar – most housebreakers or burglars ranged across a wide and varied area as they tried to cover their tracks and avoid being recognized. Being locally born, I knew the history of that area – until the early nineteenth century it had been parkland surrounding Birkbeck Manor, and the owners had sold the land for new buildings but retained the big house. That was now a fashionable hotel with sea views from its lofty situation.

The area surrounding it comprised a square mile or so of good-quality terraced houses built in white brick, fashionable at the time. The estate boasted a couple of shops – a grocer's and a butcher's – but I had no idea of the total number of houses. A rough estimate was about 250, all in neat rows on sloping ground with most having four storeys from cellar to attic. The back doors opened into individual backyards which led into a communal back alley boasting dark blue tiles upon the road surface, plus efficient drainage.

However, with the passage of only a few years, there arose a modern problem – none of the houses had a garage. As the motor car had become almost a necessity for most families, they were parked on the streets outside their owners' homes. They could not use the back alleys for parking because they were too narrow and, in any case, that was where the washing was hung out to dry and the dustbins were kept; it meant access was needed at all times. When the terraces had been built, the presence of cars had not been envisaged but once they became popular they generated a massive increase in the number of day trips. Where our ancestors had used trains and buses for lengthy holidays at Strensford, visitors now brought their own cars to town for day trips.

They arrived to find the side streets deserted by traffic during the day, with no parking restrictions. Not surprisingly, they parked their cars in those streets, some of which were very handy for the beach and town centre.

The snag was that the tourists' cars often prevented residents from parking outside their own homes when they returned from work. A system of parking permits was then adopted for the residents and this partially solved the problem, except when determined tourists ignored the signs and parked indiscriminately. This led to a considerable number of parked cars becoming nuisances and it was not surprising that some were vandalised or towed away by breakdown trucks, to be dumped in 'No Parking' areas where fines were guaranteed.

Uniformed police officers paid close attention to Birkbeck Park streets as a means of protecting vehicles and dealing with illegal parking. There is no doubt that their regular and highly visible presence led to a reduction of reported crime. As new parking areas closer to the beach and town centre were swiftly created, so the parking problems of Birkbeck Park evaporated. It seemed to happen quite suddenly. Then someone began to break into the houses and steal money.

A crime complaint from a resident of Birkbeck Park suggested an attempt to burgle his house may have been a revenge attack by a disgruntled motorist whom he had ordered to remove his car from outside his front door. But he had not recorded the registration number or the name of the car's owner; he was never traced or interviewed. The break-ins became more numerous and did not cease. In my mind, that suggested a different sort of villain at large on Birkbeck Park, someone not associated with the parking problems.

As I studied the reports and statements, it was increasingly evident that a serial burglar or housebreaker was targeting the properties: the break-ins followed an identifiable pattern and method of entry. In police jargon, they all showed the same MO (modus operandi, or method of operating), although no fingerprints or other scientific evidence had been found. Entry was by breaking the window of a cellar door at the back of each house, the cellar being below front street level and also below ground-floor level because the houses were built on steeply sloping ground. In effect, the cellars were built into the hillside with the house on top. Strensford Police had issued countless warnings and advice to the residents to lock their cellar doors and also the adjoining door which led into the kitchen, but few took any notice.

Once the window was broken, the intruder then reached inside to unlock the door and so enter the premises, not disturbing the occupants who were probably in bed and asleep. Exit was via the same route. In all cases, the premises had been thoroughly searched for cash – nothing else had been reported stolen and there was no damage to the house or its contents apart from a single broken window pane. The amounts of cash varied widely – in some cases only a few pounds had been taken, such as coins from a jam jar in the kitchen, although in one case several £5 notes were taken from a money box hidden in a bedroom drawer. Some cash had been found concealed under unused mattresses, more was taken from pantries, from under the fireside rug and even from hiding places in flower pots. The individual amounts were never very great; the stolen money seemed to be cash in hand that the householders were keeping for the proverbial rainy day, a holiday or outing to the seaside.

What did emerge was that no one had set eyes on the culprit. There was absolutely no description for us to work on. That was very odd, I felt. Despite widespread police inquiries, no witnesses had been traced. That suggested the crimes had been committed during the hours of darkness when few people were on the streets. And the singular puzzling fact was that these break-ins had not occurred in other parts of the town – that suggested a local villain with a good knowledge of the houses and the movements of their occupants.

From time to time, observations by uniformed police and detectives had taken place but with a limited number of officers to draw upon, particularly in a busy holiday resort like Strensford, nothing was achieved. However, it was significant that no crimes had been committed while they were on duty in Birkbeck Park.

The time of the alleged offences was also significant. A person who broke into a dwelling house of another between 9 p.m. and 6 a.m. with intent to steal or commit any other felony therein was guilty of burglary. If the break-in occurred outside those hours, then it was classified as housebreaking.

Burglary and sacrilege – when a person broke into or stole from a church – were considered significantly more serious than housebreaking and sometimes, because an accurate time of the break-in could not be ascertained or proved, the crime was downgraded to housebreaking. It looked less serious on Home Office returns. (Later, the Theft Act of 1968 redefined what were known as 'the breaking offences' and listed most under the single crime of burglary.)

Another dodge was to record attempted burglaries or housebreakings as malicious damage. This could occur where the criminal had damaged, say, a door or window frame with a tool like a chisel or crowbar but failed to gain entry – again, this was a lesser offence on the statistics sheets. The commission of lots of very serious crimes – felonies as they were then called – suggested the police were inefficient, so it seemed sensible to police statisticians to keep the crime figures as low as possible. It made it appear we were doing a good job, but the downside was that it indicated fewer officers were required to keep the peace, and so the opportunities for promotion were reduced. What was really needed was a constantly high crime rate!

Those crimes at Birkbeck Park could not be categorized as burglaries if the breaking in could not be proved to have occurred during the hours of darkness; consequently most were recorded as housebreakings.

Or was the damage to the door window merely malicious damage, and the missing money nothing more than theft by someone living in the house or a guest or even a mistake by the householder? Or even an insurance fiddle of some kind?

I found myself pondering the strangeness of these reports – and then I remembered something from one of my recent patrols in uniform.

CHAPTER 3

FROM MY EARLY days in uniform, I recalled a series of broken windows at Birkbeck Park. The damage had occurred over a period of a few weeks and was dealt with by the uniform branch because there was no apparent crime. They were not classified as attempted burglaries or housebreakings, but were regarded as random acts of vandalism, probably committed by someone coming home from the pub late at night. Certainly the cellar door windows at the rear parts of the Birkbeck Park terraces were vulnerable from passing vandals, especially during the hours of darkness.

At that time, this type of minor damage was classified as a misdemeanour which could be dealt with by a magistrates' court if the accused consented, and consequently such offences were not recorded as crimes. CID officers did not investigate them although they did inquire into forms of serious damage such as arson and attacks on, inter alia, specified buildings, bridges, mines, factories, rivers, roads, railways, canals and other locations.

There weren't many reports of minor damage – people tended not to report small incidents – but while parading for duty we had, on occasions, been briefed about apparently motiveless but more serious acts on the Birkbeck estate, especially at night. When briefed before our overnight patrols, we had been instructed to look out for likely perpetrators especially after the pubs turned out but also during the early hours of the darker mornings. Night patrols were alerted because the acts appeared to be the work of someone objecting to having to get out of bed early. Several householders had firmly stated their cellar door windows had been secure when they had gone to bed – then found the cellar door window broken next morning with nothing apparently stolen and no further damage.

Most cellars were used as coal houses or for storage of items not wanted upstairs in the house – outdoor brushes and shovels, for example, dustbins and old chairs and discarded furnishings that might come in useful one day even if used for firewood. The cellars were useful and had a multiplicity of uses.

Some had been adapted as wash houses or water closets (WCs) but in those cases there was an internal flight of steps that led to the ground floor of the house directly above, a lockable inner door providing the necessary security. That door opened into the back kitchen. At the time, and especially now, I wondered how many householders had regularly checked that that inner door was secure? Some of the reported thefts had occurred because internal doors had not been locked overnight. Once inside, a stealthy thief could explore and search the ground floor without rousing sleeping occupants and, of course, the thieves also needed an escape route.

It became clear that I needed to know more about those acts of damage, particularly when they had *not* involved thefts. Were all perpetrated by the same person? Did they conform to a recognizable pattern, say, their times of occurrence or the method used to smash the windows? Particular streets, perhaps? And why were no fingerprints or other evidence left at the scenes? I might find some answers in our local crime statistics.

I decided to speak to Sergeant Jim Kilner, the officer in

charge of administrative matters in Strensford Police Station. Not surprisingly known as Jim Jar, even though he might not be related to the famous jar manufacturer, he was a lanky individual with wisps of ginger hair growing from odd places on an otherwise bald head. His ears sprouted hairs and there were freckles on his face. He wore spectacles that perched on the end of his nose as if defying gravity, and he looked more like an absent-minded university professor than a policeman.

A non-operational sergeant in his early fifties (that is, he worked in an office and did not undertake patrol duties), his responsibility was entirely administrative but he wore uniform which meant he could be called upon if an emergency arose where lots of officers were required, such as a major train crash, aircraft crash, a fire at one of the large hotels on the seafront or a flood.

His secretary, a young civilian woman called Beryl Baxter ('Two Bs' for short), also worked as secretary for Superintendent Askey, but having two bosses did not appear to faze her. Beryl smiled as I entered while Jim Jar peered at me over his spectacles.

'So what brings the might of the CID to my humble office?' he asked. 'Are you seeking expenses, Rhea?'

'No, Sergeant, I'm after facts and figures.'

'What sort of facts and figures? Has Tom Latimer sent you here on an undercover operation, or are you checking for more stolen raincoats?'

'Neither, Sergeant. I want to know about incidents of malicious damage in the Birkbeck Park area. I believe the completed stats forms are kept in your office.'

'That's a bit of good detective work, Rhea, yes, they are. Explain to Beryl and she will find them for you. Am I allowed to ask why you want those? You've only been with CID for half a morning. Incidents of minor malicious damage don't usually interest our divisional sleuths.'

'I think there might be a link ...'

'Not with stolen raincoats, surely?'

I could see it was going to take a while for my miraculous raincoat recovery to be overlooked, so I answered, 'I never know what I might find in a thief's house, Sergeant. Maybe a wardrobe full of raincoats? This is just the beginning.'

'Beryl will dig the files out. Good hunting, Rhea.' The phone on his desk rang; it was Superintendent Askey summoning him for discussion. When he'd gone, Beryl located the file and handed it to me.

'You'd better take it into the muster room,' she advised with wisdom and a nice smile. 'Sergeant Kilner doesn't like others doing their work in his office.' And so I left.

It didn't take long to discover that there had been several reported cases of damage to cellar door windows during the past year in Birkbeck Park. Not exactly a crime wave but worrying none the less. I discovered that none was accompanied by a report of property or cash being stolen; consequently my immediate reaction was that the criminal had smashed the cellar window but the door had been sufficiently well locked and sturdy to prevent illegal entry. It had been recorded as damage. None of the break-ins had been through the kitchen door. The outcome was a smashed window pane with no fingerprints traced at the scene. Clearly the CID and the uniform branch worked quite independently.

Then I noted that the method of smashing the glass had not been placed on record. Had the low-situated windows been kicked in? With no fingerprints being recorded, it did seem that the glass had been broken by a weapon or tool of some kind. The handle of a chisel, a hammer, a stone, an elbow or even a foot covered with a heavy shoe or boot? But what could be the motive for merely smashing the small windows? Surely a search for money was the answer?

I must admit I began to question these reports. Had some victims of nothing more than smashed windows reported fictitious crimes in an attempt to claim insurance money? Such tactics have been known.

In other words, had no genuine burglaries or housebreakings actually been committed? Or were all these cases of 'damage only' nothing more than juvenile acts of vandalism? Kids smashing windows for a laugh? I came to the conclusion that there could be more to these cases than was immediately evident. I made careful notes of the malicious damage cases, detailing the date, time and place they had occurred. The respective householders' names were listed and I noticed that no names of suspects were given. None had been interviewed. The identity of any suspected window-breaker or teams of breakers therefore remained a mystery. Armed with this information, I returned to the CID office with some suspicions already forming in my mind.

'I thought you'd got lost, Nick,' said DS Latimer, frowning. 'Had you forgotten your warrant card or something?'

'No, nothing like that.' I explained what I had been doing. He appeared pleased if a little puzzled by my enthusiasm.

When I had finished my summary, DS Latimer pursed his lips and said, 'If you take my advice, Nick, don't waste precious time on those cases. You'll never get a conviction without catching chummy in the act of breaking in, or in possession of the stolen cash or a housebreaking tool of some kind. And if you did catch a lad in the street with a fistful of cash, how would you prove it had been stolen from any of those houses? Unless the householders had noted the serial number of the notes or marked the cash in some particular way, you'd not be able to prove anything. A denial from the thief is what you'd expect – and what you'd get. In other words, Nick, spending time and effort trying to solve such small crimes is a waste of police time.'

'I thought that was our job—'

'It is but our job is riddled with rules and regulations, procedures and case law, all contriving to prevent us doing our job properly and keeping crime down. The only chance of nicking that particular window-breaking villain is to catch him in the act, and, realistically speaking, that could only be a uniformed copper on night patrol who happened to be lurking in the shadows when chummy broke the window.'

'And waiting for him to emerge with the stolen goods?' I asked.

'You'd still have to prove the cash in his possession had come from that house, Nick.'

'Worth a try, though?'

'Worth a try,' he sighed. 'So is this the only file you've looked at?'

'So far, yes.'

'Right, well. Forget those broken windows for now, but keep them at the back of your mind. Sooner or later, there'll be another report and I'll despatch you to deal with it. But right now, I've another crime for you to solve – it was committed less than five minutes ago so you can be on the scene in minutes and hot on the trail. You might even chalk up your first arrest as a detective!'

'I hope so, but who is the injured person?' I asked. We used the term 'injured person' for the victim of a crime. It was one of the curious old words that police forces tended to use and it meant someone who had been wronged or offended by an injustice. 'PC Alf Ventress,' he told me. 'He's the victim. He was on cycle patrol from nine o'clock this morning, doing a circuit or two of Strensford including the suburbs. He rested his bike against the harbour railings to pursue some inquiries in a nearby café and minutes later found it gone. That's his story.'

'His own bike, was it?'

'No, the county bicycle. The official police cycle for Strensford. Issued by the Police Authority for our use in patrolling the town.'

'How embarrassing for Alf!' I sympathized. 'Was it his fault?'

'He can't wriggle out of this one, Nick, he should have taken more care of it.'

'I'll go and look for it,' I offered. 'Have we a description?'

'Good for you! It's big, black and a gent's sturdy Raleigh fitted with a bell, Sturmey-Archer three speed gears, rear pannier, lights back and front all in working order and under the bottom bracket is its police number – 2736. That means it was issued to us on the 2nd July 1936 so it's done a fair mileage in the last twenty years or so but the tyres and tubes are still in good condition and everything is in working order. All we want you to do, Nick, is find it. It's the ideal case for a budding sleuth! You'd never think anyone would be daft enough to steal an official police bike ...'

'Maybe it was a joke?'

'Joke or no joke, Nick, it's missing. It's been taken without authority and that makes it larceny in our books. And we don't want the press getting hold of this tale; they'd make us look like right idiots, especially Alf.'

'So where is he now?' I asked.

'Looking for the bike, I hope! Making inquiries is the official term.'

'Which café did he visit?' I asked. 'I've got to start somewhere.'

'If you can find a raincoat two years after it was nicked, then you should be able to find a police bike that was stolen five minutes ago. Alf was in Sea View Café near the harbour when it vanished. It was leaning against the harbour rails just opposite.'

'I'll do my best,' I promised.

I hurried down to the harbourside, a walk of about fifteen minutes, and went into Sea View Café. I knew the proprietor, Steve Handley – it was one of the regular places where policemen on patrol could spend a few minutes out of the public eye, enjoying a mug of tea and a sit down in the back room.

'Hi, Nick.' He beamed jovially. 'Looking for Alf?'

'I am, I'm told he's had the bike stolen.'

'Right. He leant it against those harbour railings right opposite and popped in here for a quick cuppa. The bike vanished when he was inside. He happened to look outside and noticed it had gone.'

'Who'd nick a police bike?' I asked. 'They're too easily identified … no bike thief would do that, would they? It must be a holiday-maker or visitor …'

'Or joker?'

'One of the town sergeants years ago was a joker, and if he thought the cycle patrol officer was sneaking time off for a quick cuppa in here, he'd secretly remove the bike to make the constable think it had been stolen. On another occasion, the office duty constable fell asleep at his desk on night duty, and the sergeant came in to find him snoring his head off with all the doors open. So he picked up the office typewriter and hid it in another room. Then he returned and walked in noisily to find the constable now wide awake. "All correct?" he asked. "All correct, Sergeant," responded the constable. "So where is the office typewriter? It's been stolen while you were asleep, lad …" He learned a hard lesson that night but there've been a few officers with embarrassing confessions to make – absent from their beats chatting up pretty women or placing bets on the Grand National. So, could this be a joke against Alf?' I asked.

'I can't rule it out but I don't think the town sergeant

– Blaketon, isn't it? – would do such a thing to poor Alf. I think the bike has genuinely been stolen, Nick.'

'Any ideas about that?'

'I noticed a maroon-coloured open-backed lorry parked there moments after Alf came in here. A local scrappy, I think.'

'Name? Do you know his name?'

'Sorry, no. I think he comes from some remote village on the moors every so often, collecting scrap from the shipyard and other places like garages.'

'Did you note the lorry's number?'

'No but it's got black front mudguards and there was a large grey dog sitting in the front seat; it was a Morris Commercial truck but I couldn't guess its year of registration. Quite old, though, I'd say.'

'So which way did he go from here?'

'I'd say the shipyard. I saw him leave and go over the bridge.'

'Will he still be there?'

'I'd say so; he does a lot bargaining, so one of my regular customers tells me. Quite a lot of manufacturers and other businesses leave their waste metal at the shipyard, by arrangement, and this chap comes to collect it once a month or so.'

'Thanks, Steve. So where did Alf Ventress go?'

'He said he was going to report it at the police station and explain that he wasn't feeling too well. He's worried he might be disciplined …'

'Oh, crumbs! Right, I'm off to the shipyard.'

'It's quite a walk,' Steve reminded me.

'It's time we had bikes issued to all the patrolling officers!' I grumbled.

'Not if folks go around nicking them!' laughed Steve as I left.

I prayed that the culprit and his truck were still at the shipyard's waste metal site but as I was hurrying across the harbour bridge, I saw a distinctive maroon truck with black front mudguards. It was crossing the bridge towards me and so, forgetting I wasn't in uniform, I leapt into the middle of the road and raised my hand to force it to a halt. It did so and the driver stuck his head out of his cab window and bellowed:

'What in the name of the great Beelzebub do you think you're doing, giving me heart attacks like that! Leaping in front of loaded lorries on the move could seriously damage your health, young man. It's a good job my brakes worked!'

'I want to search your truck.'

'Here?'

'Where else?'

'We're holding traffic up …'

'*You're* holding traffic up,' I accused him.

'So, if it's not a stupid question, who are you?'

'Detective Constable Rhea.' I tried to sound experienced and important.

'Then get on with it! The native drivers are getting restless. Horns are being hooted. What are you looking for?'

'A stolen pedal cycle, a black Raleigh.'

'You mean Alf Ventress's police bike?'

'Yes, that's the one.'

'Then look no further, Mr Detective, it's in the back of my truck.'

'So you admit stealing it?'

'No, I don't. I found it leaning against the harbour railings and said to myself, "Claude, old lad, if you don't take that police bike into protective custody, somebody will nick it." So I put it into the back of my truck and I'm heading for the cop shop!'

'A neat story. I'll come with you.'

And so I opened the passenger door as a grey dog leapt about excitedly and tried to lick me to death.

'Down, Alfred!' bawled the driver, adding for my benefit, 'He's only a pup but when's he's fully grown, he'll be trained to eat police officers.'

'Have you got a licence for him?' I asked.

'He doesn't need one, he's not six months old yet.'

'But you'll get one when he is six months old?' I added. 'That's if you can tell how old he is.'

'I'll have to ask his mother.' He grinned as I settled in the seat and directed him to the police station. We set off with a lot of noise as he told me, 'Or his dad. His dad was called Alfred. All my dogs are called Alfred, it runs in the family.'

'What's your name and address?' I asked as we approached the police station in Wellridge Mount. 'Are you an Alfred?'

'No, I'm Claude Jeremiah Greengrass, Hagg Bottom, Aidensfield,' he said, then added, 'I can't give my date of birth because I'm too old to remember it.'

And so I delivered the bike to the police station and went in to inform the duty sergeant, Oscar Blaketon, of my actions. 'Greengrass took it, you say? For safe-keeping? If you believe that, you'll believe anything, Rhea. The first rule of being a good police officer either in uniform or in plain clothes, is never to believe a word Greengrass says.'

'You know him?' I asked.

'Remind me to tell you about him when you've got a spare fortnight,' said Blaketon. 'The bosses are considering posting me to my own sectional police station at Ashfordly, just so that I can keep an eye on Greengrass and his antics.'

And so I went upstairs to inform DS Latimer of my actions. Unfortunately, I hadn't yet made any arrests or discovered who was breaking those cellar door windows.

CHAPTER 4

When I reported to DS Latimer in his office and told him my story, he said I'd done a good job but warned me that Claude Jeremiah Greengrass required close observation if the crime figures of the entire North Riding of Yorkshire were to be reduced.

'He's a one-man crime wave,' he told me. 'He tours in that old truck, scouring the countryside and taking all manner of metal things that appear to have been discarded as junk. In fact, much of it may have been left out for a reason – like Alf Ventress's police bike. If you hadn't caught Greengrass and accompanied him to the police station, that bike would have vanished and been stripped down to a pile of spare parts. So well done, Nick.'

'Is it always scrap iron he's looking for?'

'Not necessarily, although he is a registered old metal dealer and also a marine store dealer, hence his trips to Strensford from his yard on the moors near Aidensfield. If you know anybody who wants an old anchor to decorate their front garden, have a word with Claude and he'll find one but he might not tell you where it came from. He has his uses but he's a cunning and slippery operator, Nick. Watch him and never trust him.'

'Thanks, I'll remember that. I've a friend living here, an old schoolmate, and he told me about leaving an old broken-down oven on the street, hoping a scrap merchant would take it away but nobody did. So he put a notice on it saying "For Sale £12" and someone took it away.'

'A good ploy! Probably it was Greengrass, thinking it was valuable. Right, Nick, so you've abandoned the broken window vandal inquiry?'

'Let's say I've taken your advice and am not actively pursuing those inquiries at the moment, Sergeant. I shall not ignore them, though, my conscience won't let me, but in the meantime I thought I'd have another look at the file you gave me. To see what other cases might benefit from a little extra attention.'

'There's always a selection of nuisance crimes, Nick, all undetected, and all needing to be revisited. You might have a look at the "Damage to cars" files.'

'Vandalism, is it?'

'More than that. There's always a crime involved which is why we in CID are making inquiries. Cars parked overnight on some of the streets are being attacked and valuables stolen. People are daft enough to leave things in their cars, openly on view. The thieves leave no fingerprints and no other evidence. It doesn't seem to be a form of protest about them parking outside somebody's house, it's more a case of stealing untraceable valuables from the vehicles. And, Nick, it's not restricted to this town. It's occurring in beauty spots on the moors and near the coast; people park their cars to go for long walks and leave things on show – cameras, binoculars, even jackets and handbags with money in pockets or wallets. Sometimes we can't believe how careless they are, inviting thieves to help themselves.'

'So it's not only money that's targeted?'

'Anything of value, Nick, including money. Holidaymakers are particularly vulnerable and leave amounts of cash visible but also other things like tennis rackets, clothing, portable radio sets and even hardback books. All these things have been stolen, but another rich seam of theft are cases belonging to travelling salesmen who leave all sorts in their vehicles – samples of everything from shoes to household goods like electric whisks and cutlery sets. The simple message is "anything of value on view in a motor vehicle is a target for thieves".'

'Our crime prevention officers tell us that all the time, don't they?'

'They do, but no one takes much notice until it happens to them. Our worst case locally was a briefcase full of samples to show to jewellers – gold and silver pieces, even diamonds and pearls, and so on – and it was nicked. I expect the car driver got sacked for that carelessness.'

'No arrests then?'

'Very few – like many in our files, that jewellery thief has not been caught. Your first CID arrest is unlikely to be one of those thieves: they're far too slippery.'

'It seems that one knew what he was looking for!'

'Or else it was pot luck. Luck plays a big part in crime.'

'So how do they break into the cars?'

'Usually by smashing the quarter lights on the driver's side, reaching in and unlocking the door. That's a very common means of breaking into a vehicle – most have their quarter lights broken which gives access to the door locks. The villains either wear gloves or use cloths to open the doors from inside the cars – and leave no prints.'

'More broken windows?' I queried.

'You're not linking these with those cellar door windows, are you? And before you answer, you can rule out Greengrass. Committing that kind of crime is just not his scene. He'll nick things left out at night near houses, pubs, factories and so on, and do dodgy deals like many petty thieves do, but he's not a housebreaker or a burglar. And he's not violent.'

'It would be interesting to see exactly where the attacked cars were parked,' I suggested. 'If they were anywhere near the Birkbeck Park area, there may be a link, a phantom window smasher who nicks small saleable items that can't be traced ...'

'Nick, it never occurred to me or any of my team that there might be such a link with the window breaker but I must admit it sounds feasible. It's the same MO – smash the window with a blunt instrument without leaving any prints or other evidence, reach inside to open a lock. All right, delve into those files and let me know your reaction, then go out and arrest the thief or thieves.'

Over the next few days in quiet periods, I searched the back files and extracted several reports of cars and one or two vans being broken into. Some contained expensive tools – plumbing and carpentry mainly – and were stolen over a long period but only two of the crimes had been committed in the Birkbeck Park area. Others were around the town, a long way apart, and I could see no discernible pattern. One was on the northern outskirts, probably about a mile away, but as I had no transport I settled for a case much nearer home.

It was 22 Kerngate in the east of the town beneath the cliffs upon which stood the imposing lighthouse complex and coastguard's offices. It took me about ten minutes to walk there and I found the property without difficulty. It was on the main street with a parking area at one side and I noted the car in question was parked outside. The crime had been committed some ten days earlier and I noticed its quarter light had been repaired. Before setting off, I had made a note of the occupant's name – Geoffrey Preston – and now I hammered on the front door, there being no bell or knocker.

After a few moments, I heard the door being unlocked and

a very tall, smartly dressed man in casual clothes with a thick mop of white hair greeted me. 'Yes?'

'Mr Geoffrey Preston?' I asked.

'I am and who are you?'

'Detective Constable Rhea from Strensford CID.' I had momentarily forgotten I was not in uniform, which is always a great ice-breaker when introducing oneself, especially to a complete stranger. Instead, I showed him my warrant card and he nodded.

'So how can I help?' he asked without inviting me inside.

'I've been tasked to review some unsolved criminal cases, Mr Preston, and am interested in the recent theft from your car.'

'Oh, right. Well, you'd better come in. I'm an architect and I work mainly from home but for that I can spare you a few minutes.' He led me into a comfortable lounge overlooking the street, settled me on a sofa and asked, 'So how can I help? Clearly you have not caught the thief.'

'Not yet.' I tried to sound confident and did not wish to tell him I was a very new detective. 'I'm trying to establish whether there are links between your case and others that have been reported. I'm particularly interested in a series of crimes where cellar windows on the Birkbeck Park estate have been targeted. There have also been several raids on assorted vehicles – cars and vans – two of which were on the Birkbeck Park estate. Their windows were broken too, which enabled the thief to open a door without leaving any evidence.'

'I had no idea there were other instances like mine, Mr Rhea. I thought I had been targeted by someone who knew what I was carrying in my briefcase. I must admit I thought some of my acquaintances may have been involved. Maybe not, in view of what you have told me.'

'Our report says you had about £120 in notes stolen. It was a lot of money to keep in your car, Mr Preston.'

'It wasn't on view, if that's what you're going to suggest. It was in a pocket of my briefcase, an internal pocket. I always have it handy because I never know when or where I have to spend a night in a hotel or buy a late meal and so forth. I always carry a reserve of cash for emergencies. No one would know it was there.'

'Yet you left it in the car? Unattended?'

'A foolish thing to do! I realize that now and it was entirely my own fault. I was late home that evening and was very tired after a long day and a long journey. I forgot to bring my briefcase in. It's probably the only time I've done that so it's almost as if the thief knew it contained cash.'

'But the briefcase wasn't removed?'

'No, it had been opened and left where it was, on the rear seat. Your scenes of crime team said there were no fingerprints or other evidence. Cash only was taken and I am sufficiently worldly wise to know it cannot be identified as mine unless I had recorded the serial numbers of the notes, which I had not.'

'What interests me, Mr Preston, is that the break-ins were via the quarter lights of cars and vans. That method is very similar to housebreakings or burglaries on the Birkbeck Park estate; the interior bolts or locks can be manipulated to open the doors. In those cases, small panes of glass were smashed in cellar door windows, and the bolts or Yale locks inside were then opened to admit the thief.'

'I'm familiar with those streets and houses.' Preston smiled. 'You'd never smash those small panes with a bare fist or elbow. You'd need a hammer of some kind. And I speak as an architect who is interested in the security of buildings. Modern glass is much tougher than hitherto, I make good use of it in ground-floor windows I design. And small panes are the most difficult to break.'

'The houses on Birkbeck Park are quite old ones, Mr Preston.'

'Yes, they are, but not ancient. Early nineteenth century if my knowledge is correct. Their small panes will be tough to break, even those made at that time, especially in ground-floor rooms. Your break-and-entry merchant must be using a hammer or heavy tool of some kind – and he would need to remove the sharp pointed pieces before inserting his hand and arm. That would take time so it he was obviously confident he was not going to be discovered at his nefarious work.'

'Can you see a link between those cellar windows and car quarter lights?' I asked.

'Only that both use small panes of glass, Mr Rhea. That would be a factor but as the perpetrator uses an instrument of some kind to smash the glass, it suggests some kind of special knowledge.'

'Special knowledge? I don't follow,' I admitted.

'Well, he – or she – might have been to a lecture about the special qualities of some glass and might know the theory of its behaviour in certain circumstances. The manufacture of glass is getting more sophisticated as each year passes and the finished product may be much tougher than ordinary glass, if you follow. The older the glass, the more fragile it is.'

'I'm thinking of burglars and housebreakers ...'

'And I'm thinking of plumbers, carpenters and others who might have a deeper knowledge of glass not common in ordinary people.'

'It doesn't take a specialized knowledge of glass to smash it with a hammer,' I replied.

'It might in some cases,' he said quietly.

'Sorry, I'm misjudging you—'

'No problem! I have fitted safety glass to many of the buildings I've designed – some of it will withstand a severe hammering before fracturing, especially small panes in vulnerable places, or where security is vital. Whoever smashed those windows, whether on my car or in those terraced houses, needed to achieve his purpose with the minimum of noise and in the shortest time whilst also avoiding injuries that might leave blood or fingerprints.'

'We had some attempted burglaries or housebreakings where the burglars broke the windows but did not follow up with entry to the premises,' I told him. 'That's quite common.'

'Maybe their efforts made too much noise or they cut themselves; there can be all sorts of reasons for abandoning illegal entry to houses or business premises. I think, with all due respect, you need to speak to someone in the building trade, a plumber or glazier perhaps, to learn the current properties of both security glass and earlier glazing. If someone with specialized knowledge is breaking into houses or even cars, and stealing money and goods that can't be identified, it sounds to me, Mr Rhea, that there is a very clever criminal operating in the town. One who is prepared to rapidly abort his efforts if he senses danger or discovery.'

'That equates with some attacks on houses elsewhere, Mr Preston, which appear to be attempts to break in through windows but were aborted before the criminal got into the premises. They're listed as damage.'

'I think that lends support to my theory, Mr Rhea. You have a criminal who is stealthily moving around the town whilst being careful not to be seen or caught in action. This is emphasized by his theft of cash and objects that the loser can't identify as his or her property. Burglary by stealth in other words.'

'Our night patrols are aware of these activities but so far the culprit has avoided arrest.'

'Police officers cannot be everywhere at once, Mr Rhea. Even I know that. Clearly he is skilled at avoiding them. But how do criminals know where and when to attack houses, cars and other places? Is it instinct, pot luck, experience, skill, information gleaned beforehand … or what?'

'If we knew that, our crime figures would show a huge surge in arrests and convictions, Mr Preston, but we're not thought readers or prophets. I think a lot of luck enters the story – and the criminals can recognize wealth and quality when they see it. It's not all luck that some of their raids are successful. Anyway, thanks for your time, I've enjoyed this chat.'

'I hope you found it helpful, Mr Rhea.' He rose to his feet. 'Now I must let you go as I am expecting a client. Keep in touch. I would like to know when, where or if you catch this phantom felon.'

'I'll let you know when it happens,' was all I could promise as I left him.

I decided to walk back to the police station, half a mile or so away, and that meant crossing the harbour bridge which provided a panoramic view of the town's older houses clustered together on the cliffs almost like housemartins' nests. The town was busy with tourists and regular visitors, and the fishing fleet was at sea, the harbour now busy with cabin cruisers, yachts and leisure vessels. I was thinking I was blessed to have such an interesting job in such an interesting place; there was history and tradition here, and I was reminded of that as I walked past the ancient White Griffin Inn, said to have been a favourite of Charles Dickens and the setting for many of his yarns.

I recalled my schooldays in this town and how, on one occasion some years ago, our class was studying the works of Dickens, *Oliver Twist* in particular, and our teacher felt that a visit to this old inn would help us to absorb something of the atmosphere of those times. It was a nice visit, the landlord giving us all a sandwich and a soft drink, and showing us some of the woodwork and artefacts that dated from Dickens' time. One was an atmospheric sketch of Fagin, framed and displayed on the lounge wall.

And now, as a fledgling detective trying to catch modern Fagins, a possibility entered my head. I hurried back to the CID office.

CHAPTER 5

My hurried walk through the town allowed a few minutes of uninterrupted thinking time. As I was not in uniform, no one stopped me to ask directions, to recommend a café or to ask the way to Scarborough or Middlesbrough. When I got to the CID office I wanted to check on a few salient facts about the timing of the break-ins or even those cases of damage only but my energetic walk revived memories of my uniform patrolling in Strensford. I found myself recalling some of my uniform patrols when on night duty.

As raw recruits, once our three months' training at the District Training Centre was complete, we were posted to a town to gain on-the-job experience under supervision and guidance. One of my first training exercises was to spend a month on night duty patrol in the town under the tuition of a senior constable. The main purpose was to acquaint us with the geography of Strensford, with its complicated street layout interspaced with ginnels (passages), but also its relationship with surrounding towns and villages. There was also the town's busy harbourside and beach culture, a lesson in itself.

We had to know the whereabouts and activities of Strensford's council offices, shops, cafés, nightclubs, pubs, likely trouble spots, amusement arcades, dogs' homes and animal shelters, slaughter houses, betting shops, pawnbrokers, public car parks, graveyards and churches, schools, factories and explosives stores. In addition we had to know where to find the rough areas, the smart residential areas, cinemas, theatres and public halls, hospitals and surgeries, garages with lifting equipment, places that opened or were staffed all night or at odd hours such as the fire station, ambulance station, coastguard station, lifeboat house, railway station, swing-bridge operator, taxi ranks, newspaper publisher/printer, nearby military establishments and more.

We also had to know the home addresses of our uniformed colleagues in case they had to be called out in emergencies. None had telephones at home in those days so a knock on the door was necessary. In short, we had to know as much as possible about our town in case there was an emergency, large or small, but also to efficiently carry out our normal duties even if it involved nothing more than answering questions from tourists. It was not easy trying to remember all the necessary places and purposes – that would come with experience – but it was surprising how a quiet walk in the dead of night did impress itself upon our memories.

I recalled my first impression of nightlife in Strensford, as seen from the viewpoint of a patrolling constable. The most resilient memory is of the sheer volume of activity that occurred while most of the townspeople were asleep.

For example, the herring fishing fleet was obliged to operate when the prevailing tides and weather permitted and so fishermen worked lots of long and different hours. Incoming fishing fleets from elsewhere in Britain, including Scotland, or overseas from Holland and other maritime nations, also fished off this coast and unloaded their catches on the dockside. As always, it occurred when the weather and tides permitted. On those occasions, the harbourside was awash with lights, noise, people, trawlers, goods vehicles and crates of fresh herring measured in crans. As a young man who had grown up in the area and attended school in this town, I had no previous experience of this activity but for many of the townspeople, it was part of their lives and therefore not worthy of their comment.

The man who worked in a tiny cabin at one end of the swing bridge also worked odd hours that were dictated by the tides.

He had to be in his cabin two hours before and two hours after each high tide to open the bridge and allow vessels of all shapes and sizes to pass from the lower harbour into the calmer waters of the upper and vice versa. With two high and two low tides roughly every twenty-four hours at ever-changing times albeit with about an hour's progressive difference to each individual tide per day, his sleep patterns must have been chaotic.

Despite that, he was constantly cheerful and would always share a flask of coffee with the night-patrolling constables. He enjoyed our companionship during those long lonely hours.

Post Office workers also arrived early to sort the mail, which came either by early train or sometimes by motor vehicle. All the parcels and letters had to be sorted for that morning with emphasis upon early deliveries to business addresses and commercial or municipal offices, not forgetting the hospital. Domestic deliveries could take second place!

We rarely saw groups of nurses, doctors or ward orderlies heading for work because the hospital lay on the edge of town and it had its own live-in accommodation for nurses and other staff. Likewise, the fire station had overnight accommodation where firemen could rest until an emergency aroused them; the ambulance workers had a similar system.

Other groups of very early-morning workers included window cleaners and bakers. A team of four window cleaners began work in the town centre around 3.30 a.m. Monday to Saturday, the early start being due to them wishing to clean all their shop and office customers' windows before the staff arrived and customers were active. By the time the office and shop workers arrived, the cleaners would be in the suburbs, busy with house windows. I now realize how hard those people worked.

In addition to small cafés and bread shops, the town had two major restaurants, each with shops that sold a range of bread, pies and cakes. Their staff arrived from about 4 a.m. to produce fresh products for sale at 8.30 a.m. onwards.

All the workers I've mentioned were quite visible to a patrolling constable – they arrived by car, motorbike, pedal cycle or on foot, and would exchange greetings with any patrolling constable they encountered. I began to realize the town was as busy at night as it was during the day. The only things missing at night were tourists, although some seemed to wait until the pubs and clubs closed before making their presence known, sometimes in an objectionable and noisy manner. From time to time, police officers would have to bring their celebrations to an abrupt conclusion.

But there was another category of early-morning worker, some of whom moved silently through the darkness, albeit aided by a modicum of street lighting, as they travelled to work. They arrived at different times; some very early ones used pedal cycles and others came by motor car or motorcycle as they headed towards what looked like a modern square tower block close to both the harbourside and the railway station. It had a spacious car park and I think the six-storey tower was constructed of wood and metal – certainly, it did not look like either a stone or brick building but it had a lot of windows and a loading bay at the base.

It was not a handsome building but I guessed it was extremely functional. Many vehicles arrived in the early hours to deposit their loads and as the morning progressed, the doors of the loading bay were eventually lifted and a row of vans could be discerned inside.

They were awaiting their final loads before rushing off to locations in town or on the outskirts. This business was open seven days a week, only closing on Christmas Day and Good Friday.

This was the Strensford newspaper and magazine distribution centre, which ensured that all the local newspaper shops, rural stores and other outlets received their newspapers and magazines in time for their morning customers, sometimes as early as 5.30 a.m. The local newspaper, the *Strensford Gazette*, had its own offices close to the swing bridge, part of which was a printing press which produced its weekly paper every Friday. It also printed a range of booklets, pamphlets and other printed matter during the week. On Fridays its van brought copies of the *Gazette* for distribution around the outskirts of the town and rural areas. National papers and magazines arrived by rail at the nearby railway station and were also carried into the tower block for local distribution.

This was a well-organized operation that continued throughout the year, often without Mr Ordinary Man knowing how his newspaper arrived on his breakfast table with yesterday's late news after being printed overnight in London, Manchester or elsewhere. In Strensford's case, most of the newspaper shops sent their paper boys and girls directly to the distribution centre where they collected their allocation of papers for immediate delivery instead of taking them to a newsagent's or other shop to be sorted. They were delivered direct from the distribution centre, which meant avid readers would be presented with a very early edition through their letterbox; to collect copies for counter sales, the shops made their own arrangements, some hiring taxis.

As I stood and stared at this edifice in daylight, I realized that many of the young lads and lasses – mainly schoolchildren – who found their way here did so in darkness, particularly in the winter months, which extended from late autumn into early spring.

Recalling my uniform patrols in Strensford, I knew that only one shop in the Birkbeck Park estate sold newspapers and magazines. It was like a village store in that it provided almost everything from food to house maintenance items. And it sold newspapers and magazines over the counter, in addition to having a delivery boy or girl, perhaps two in busy times. Those delivery lads and lasses would pass through the streets on foot in the darkness of some very early winter mornings en route to the collection point. I didn't think they would have the time to break into one of those terraced houses they passed but they might smash a cellar door window in seconds by using the right tool, then vanish into the all-embracing darkness of early morning. A hammer was not vital; merely a hammer head would be enough. And the street lights were not lit all night.

I thought of Fagin and wondered if such a paper boy could be persuaded by an adult to knock a hole through a cellar door window and then leave it, without asking why. Later, also under cover of darkness, even on another day or night, the adult might visit the same scene, enter by unlocking the cellar door and inserting his hand through the hole in the window to draw back the bolt or turn a key if there was one, taking care to avoid getting cut by the remaining glass.

If the coast was clear, he could then enter to make a swift and quiet search of the house, taking only cash and ensuring no fingerprints or evidence was left to incriminate him – or her.

As I pondered the scenario I had imagined, I realized it was quite feasible and also a cunning way of breaking into houses. It was cunning because the actual breaker, probably below the age of criminal responsibility, was not the thief; it was a team job with no fingerprints and no other clues. But there was a clue. The local shop at the end of Beech Terrace at the top of the park! I decided to divert from my original intention of heading into the CID office, and instead turned towards Birkbeck Park and its shop.

It had been constructed when the estate was built and comprised a spacious ground floor housing the public area with a flat above for the owners. It was privately owned and a very successful enterprise, selling everything from groceries to hardware via wines, spirits and beers, fruit and vegetables, greetings cards, clothing for children and a small range of fresh meat supplied by a local butcher. From my uniform experiences, I knew the owners were Betty and Stan Milner. I wasn't sure whether they would recognize me in civilian clothes so I decided to adopt some subterfuge in my approach. I needed a story that did not throw suspicion on the paper boy or girl, or anyone else.

Mrs Milner, a homely-looking woman in her early fifties with greying hair, noticed my entry and so I went to the newspaper stand and began to search.

'Can I help, Mr Rhea?' So she *did* recognise me!

'I'm looking for the *Daily Mail*,' I explained.

'We're sold out. You might find one at WH Smith's in town.'

'It doesn't really matter, there'll probably be one at the station.'

'You're off duty, I see.' She smiled, clearly curious about my presence.

'I am, and it's nice to get out of that uniform. Actually, I'm looking for a lad, a paper boy called Terry Naylor, and a pal from work suggested I look here.'

'I don't know him but he's not in trouble, is he?'

'Oh no, nothing like that. He's the son of an old pal of mine from training school days and I'm his godfather. I forgot his birthday. Somebody said the lad was living in town with an aunt and working as a paper boy each morning. His mum isn't well and she's in hospital, and his dad's away on a police course down south.'

'Oh dear, how sad! Have you tried the distribution centre?'

'Not yet, that's my next port of call. I happened to be here so I thought you might know him.'

'Sorry, no. Our paper lad's called Ian Donovan and he lives just along this street. He's the only one we employ.'

'Well, thanks anyway. I'll ask elsewhere as you suggest. It's not all that important but if the lad's mum is ill and he's been boarded out with an aunt, he might appreciate a birthday present, even if it is late.'

'A nice thought, Mr Rhea. I hope you track him down.'

'With the help I get from people, I'm sure I will. Thanks for your part in this.'

I didn't like this kind of deviousness but sometimes it was necessary and this time it provided a good lead – the name of a paper boy. It was a small start. I could easily find the Donovan address from the electoral register and I smiled my appreciation as I left, then headed for the CID office to continue my inquiries. I now felt very optimistic. As I walked in, the place was deserted with all the Ds out on inquiries.

DI Baldwin was in his office and emerged when he heard my presence. Plump and in his mid-forties, he was always jolly and had a wonderful knack of incorporating swear words into words – one of his most often used was 'abso-bloody-lutely' and another was 'spot-bloody-on'.

'Now, young Rhea.' His broad face was wreathed in a smile. 'How's things? Enjoying learning to be a divisional sleuth?'

'I am, sir, thanks. Far better than plodding around the town harassing motorists. I'm looking into a family called Donovan—'

'Not those Donovans from Birkbeck bloody Park by any chance?'

'Yes, Beech Terrace ...'

'A family of villains, Nick, except for the mother. She's hard-working and honest, but she's crewed up with a viper's nest of baddies from the grand-bloody-father down to her husband and her four sons. Sneak thieves, the lot of 'em. Let one of 'em walk through Woolworths and he'll come out the other end with pockets full of useless stuff he's nicked without anybody seeing him. Put 'em in the bar of a pub and they'll walk out with a bottle of beer hidden somewhere. They can't help it ... *none of 'em*. Light-fingered since birth, the whole sodding crowd! They'll pinch anything that's not nailed down. We've alerted Mrs Milner in her shop on Beech Terrace, especially because one of 'em's working there as the paper lad. So how did you get involved with that tawdry lot? Sit down and tell me.'

I sat in my usual seat at the big table as I explained about the broken cellar door windows and he listened, nodding occasionally. He let me finish my tale, then asked, 'So what do you conclude from all this?'

'I wondered if a child was breaking the windows for the father to follow later, not necessarily on the same day, to enter the house to steal whatever he could.'

'The Fagin syndrome? It happens! I'd say you're right, Nick, or almost a hundred per cent right, so well done. '

'Almost right?' I queried.

'A variation might be that one of the elder boys could be the villain, bullying his kid brother to do the initial dirty work. Dad might not be the villain in these cases – it's just a cautionary thought.'

'But the thief will need to enter the premises before the broken window is discovered and repaired,' I pointed out.

'We've been watching that family, Nick, and what you say is spot on, except that entry could be days later. The way some of these folks live means they don't go down to their cellars every day. So the child punches a hole through the cellar door window with a hammer head but doesn't hang about, gets away from the scene as fast as he can to get an alibi by collecting the papers before normal folks are out of bed. You'd be surprised how many householders don't ever discover that broken window – and none have reported hearing it being broken. Bedrooms have a living area between them and the cellar, and the family visits the cellar on few occasions, usually to get scuttles of coal or collect firewood. Most enter the cellar from the kitchen, they rarely use that outer door. They can go about their normal routine for a week or more without realizing someone's knocked a hole in the cellar door window. You'd be amazed how many folks never lock the inner door from the cellar into the kitchen; they rely on the locked outer door of the cellar. All the real villain has to do is to open the cellar door in the darkness by manipulating the lock by hand or sliding back the securing bolt or bolts using a tool to avoid fingerprints, and he's in. No noise! He can search the house before people are out of bed, and an experienced thief knows where to find hidden cash.'

'So that's what's been happening?'

'We think so and I'm sure some of those raids were never discovered for weeks, if at all – some cellar doors have thick curtains over their windows so the smashed glass is often unnoticed from the inside.'

'You make it sound easy and trouble-free, sir!'

'It's not, it takes skill. And no fingerprints are left, and furthermore the stolen cash – always cash – is unidentifiable. A skilled operator is at work, Nick, which is why no one's been caught. He must have accumulated lots of cash, all tax free!'

'The perfect crime, sir?'

'No crime is perfect, Nick.'

'So what makes you think the burglar might be one of the

sons rather than the dad?'

'One of them – Benny – works on the fishing fleet that sails from our harbour; he works odd hours and often goes to work in the darkness. He nips into a house with a broken cellar door window, spends five minutes or less, and leaves silently with a fistful of cash. Who's going to suspect a man aboard a fishing boat somewhere in the North Sea? A simple scenario. And if you interview any of that clan – which we've done many times – they deny everything whilst admitting they were out and about in the early hours on their way to or from work. I might add that we checked sailing times and high-tide movements over a few months, and it does strengthen our case against the Donovans.'

'But still no proof or evidence?'

'None, Nick. Just speculation and local bloody knowledge, but that doesn't carry any weight in a court of law. There's nothing we can do to prove their guilt.'

'Except catching them in the act?'

'Ever tried catching a shadow? But yes, we do need to catch them in the act and that in turn demands manpower and long hours in unproductive observation, most of which turns out to be worthless. If we were watching in the darkness, they'd know we were there. Even if we caught them in the act, they'd never admit to the crimes and we'd have a job to prove the money in their possession had been stolen.'

'Could we wait inside the target house and arrest them on suspicion? Catch them in the act?'

'Doubtful. We need to arrest them *leaving* with identifiable stolen goods in their possession. Mere trespass in a house is not a crime but it's illegal as a civil tort, which is not a police matter.'

'So we need to set a trap!'

'We do, but that's easier said than done. But we're working on it.'

I knew the DI was speaking the truth and the good news was that attention was being paid to that rogue family; I was confident there would be a result, even if it took a long time with many hours of patient police work. I could not make an arrest solely on the intelligence and suspicion I had gathered so far. The boss was right – I could not afford to spend any more time on those crimes but I felt I had made my contribution.

And there I had to leave that inquiry. Soon afterwards another theft was reported.

'This one's for you, Nick,' said DI Baldwin, smiling. 'Someone's made a pilgrimage to the collection plate at the back of St Patrick's Church and stolen the contents.'

CHAPTER 6

THE PRIEST-IN-CHARGE OF St Patrick's Catholic Church at Strensford was Monsignor Dermot O'Leary, a sturdy figure who oozed kindness and consideration for all, whatever their faith, including non-Christians. A rather small, kindly but comforting figure of a man, he was in his late sixties with a mop of white hair and a strong Irish accent despite living in England since he was in his teens. His hobby was collecting watercolour paintings by local artists old and new, of which he possessed an encyclopaedic knowledge, and he was also a popular after-dinner speaker due to his vivid and hilarious stories of life in rural Ireland.

The young assistant priest was Father John MacDonald, a 30-year-old Scotsman who was an all-round sportsman and a fine vocalist. They both lived in St Patrick's presbytery behind the church in its town-centre location and were under the care of (and some parishioners said under the thumb of) the redoubtable Miss Carey, a native of Cornwall who had devoted her life to caring for priests. A small, fussy woman of indeterminate late-middle age, she was prepared to move to any part of England in order to follow her chosen path to heaven. She had once thought about becoming a nun but had rejected that because she felt her mission was to look after others rather than herself. No one knew Miss Carey's first name but when she spoke she commanded immediate obedience, even from the Bishop. She had a sister who was equally devoted to good causes and who had worked as a cook in a monastery with never a day off, on duty from early breakfast through to evening supper. Both Carey women saw their work as being dedicated to God. I often wondered how God would cope with them when they joined him in heaven.

There was another Catholic church in Strensford, St Joseph's at the east side of the harbour. It catered for that part of the town and its priest was the comely Father Hugo Latimer (a cousin of our detective sergeant), who loved red wine and parish parties, often excusing the happiness they generated by claiming he was reviving the Marriage at Cana where Jesus turned water into wine.

Technically he was subservient to Monsignor O'Leary at St Patrick's but seemed to run his own parish without interference from anyone either above or nearby. I was aware of these facets of the Catholic Church's modern presence in Strensford due to my own Catholicism and was on good terms with all the priests. Now, though, I was a detective constable charged with the investigation of a crime in one of our churches.

'Are you happy about tackling this one, Nick?' asked DI Baldwin. 'If not, we can find someone-bloody-else with experience and you can tag along to see how things are done or should be done!'

'I'd better do it alone, sir.' I knew I must learn to be independent and confident in my new role. 'It shouldn't be all that difficult.'

'Cash often goes missing from St Patrick's,' he told me. 'Almost always it goes from the collection plate at the back of the church. We have a relaxed attitude to this – people in real need are told that they can take money from here, no questions asked, the plate is always here and replenished regularly. It is openly displayed for people to drop in their donations too. For most of the time, the cash is safe – people don't like stealing from the house of God! But lately someone has been doing the rounds of churches across Yorkshire, pocketing the cash from those plates. There've been no break-ins or damage, just simple theft, which means the crimes are most difficult to detect.'

'Is the church open all day?'

'It is, but locked at night. When the church is open, anyone can pop in and that's our problem. No one knows who's been calling.'

'Churches have always been left available for anyone who wishes to spend a quiet moment or two in God's presence. Some are open all night,' I reminded him. 'That's not only an English custom, it's worldwide.'

'I appreciate that, Nick, but God-all-bloody-mighty can't protect all his churches and I'm afraid an increasing number of villains are entering open churches to steal whatever they can. And it's not just cash. Candlesticks, altar furnishings, silverware, paintings, cash – even statues have been stolen. Churches are rich hunting grounds for rogues, Nick. The short answer is that churches need to take more care of their own treasures.'

'I realize that things left in open containers or on display without protection are always a temptation but I have to say that Catholics believe God will take care of things.'

'Not when he's faced with the British criminal mentality accompanied by a determination to get something for nothing, Nick. I'm sure some thieves think they have a God-given right to take things that are not protected, like cash in open bowls, even if they are in churches.'

'I couldn't agree more; it seems our society is not being encouraged to be God-fearing and honest.'

'It's our problem, Nick. We are supposed to prevent crimes

as well as detect them but the only sure prevention is to conceal the cash in thief-proof containers and secure any valuables. Mark my words, Nick, based on years of experience, these crimes are going to escalate.'

'I must say our society encourages crime with so many temptations being available,' I added.

'That's the growing problem. Anywhere that gives the public open access needs to be protected against thieves, such as the growing trend for self-service in shops. And it includes churches in spite of the commandment that says "Thou shalt not steal" – that's the message the priests should be enforcing.'

'I'll see if I can persuade the local ones to give more protection to their money,' I said. 'Maybe a follow-up visit by a crime prevention officer would be a good idea?'

'We've tried that, not just with churches but with shops and department stores – anywhere that the great and nasty British public is likely to nick stuff. Most store bosses don't take a scrap of notice. In fact, they seem to think that if villains nick stuff from open displays, it confirms their appeal to shoppers.'

'So we're fighting a losing battle, sir?'

'Yes, we are, but that mustn't stop us trying. One thought, Nick. If the thief at St Patrick's has any sort of conscience, he might have confessed to one of those priests.'

'If he – or she – has the gall to steal from a church, they're not the sort who would make a confession afterwards. Besides, sir, if he or she has confessed to a priest, we'll never know. Priests cannot disclose what is told to them during confession.'

'Not even if it's a confession of murder?'

'Not even that, sir.'

'Ah, well, that's one promising-bloody-line of inquiry that's closed. All right, off you go, let me know how you get on.'

In the case of any reported crime, however minor, it is vital that the investigating officer visits the scene. It is impossible to gain a realistic impression of the crime otherwise and so I entered St Patrick's Church by the main door. Now, though, I was entering as a detective and not a member of the congregation. There were two doors to pass through before gaining entry to the nave; the first took me into the porch with its stone benches at each side and notices pinned to the boards on the side walls. The next door led into the rear of the nave where, behind the two rows of pews, stood a pair of matching tables. The table on the left behind the north aisle pews supported three collection bowls as well as piles of hymnals and handouts detailing the form of services that day. The one on the right – the south aisle – bore pamphlets and booklets which could be taken away, either buying them by putting money into a box, or by taking free copies.

I noted there was no money in any of the collecting bowls, but when I shook the wooden box that stood among the booklets, it rattled, showing that coins were among its contents. It was about the size of a shoebox with a slit in the lid, therefore easily portable. I was surprised it hadn't been stolen. A thief could easily pick it up and carry it off to break open at his leisure but it would be difficult to conceal among one's clothing. As I looked around, I realized there were no wall safes or collecting boxes built into the stonework. Hanging around the walls were religious scenes and images of saints, while the altar displayed half a dozen splendid brass candlesticks and a large brass crucifix complete with the figure of the crucified Christ. My first impressions of the scene before me were that it was all too easy to steal from this church.

As I stood alone, deep in thought and wondering how best to make this place more crime conscious, I heard a door open and saw Monsignor O'Leary entering from the vestry. There was another door leading out of the vestry directly into the presbytery, and I wondered if he was aware of my presence. I decided to alert him.

'Good morning, Monsignor,' I called in not-too-loud a voice.

He turned to look at me, somewhat short-sightedly, I thought, so I announced my name.

'Ah, Nick the policeman.' He smiled at his own interpretation of my name and began to walk towards me. 'So how can I help or is yourself seeking a moment or two of quiet prayer before God?' I loved his strong Irish accent.

'I'd like a chat,' I said, adding, 'with you. I'm here on police business.'

'Then you'd better come into the presbytery where, God willing, Miss Carey will make us a cup of coffee.'

I followed him through the vestry into the presbytery where he led me into a comfortable drawing room adorned with holy pictures and a crucifix, then he pressed a bell button on the wall. Moments later, Miss Carey, a small, slightly stooped woman with a mop of white hair and wearing a copious apron, appeared in the doorway.

'You rang, Monsignor?'

'As you can see, Miss Carey, we have a guest. Perhaps you could rustle up something for us. Coffee or tea, Nick?'

'Coffee would be nice. White with sugar.'

'Make two if you please, Miss Carey, with biscuits,' and off she went to do his bidding.

He indicated a pair of armchairs in front of the hearth, currently without a fire, and after we had settled down, he asked, 'So, Nick, how can I help the constabulary?'

'It's to do with the stolen donations,' I began.

'Stolen donations? What stolen donations?'

'From the collection plate at the back of the church.'

'I know nothing of that!'

'We received a report this morning saying there had been a theft, and so I'm here to investigate it.'

'Did they say how much had been taken?'

'We've no idea. Perhaps you could give us some kind of estimate?'

'I doubt if anyone could quote an accurate figure but the donations placed in that dish are remarkably steady, Nick. Around a couple of pounds a day plus bits and pieces of loose change, running at an average of £15 a week. Or thereabouts. But who reported this? I can assure you it was not me, and if it had been Father John he would have told me. And Philomena wouldn't have rung you.'

'Philomena?'

'Miss Carey to outsiders.' He smiled. 'She rarely uses her Christian name but I managed to discover it. So do you know who rang the police?'

'I don't, I was simply ordered to come and investigate the crime. But I can find out for you if I can use your phone.'

'Sure, help yourself, it's on the window ledge behind you.'

As I dialled the police station number, Miss Carey entered with the tray of coffee and biscuits, and placed it on a small table before us. As she was leaving, I found myself speaking to the duty officer, PC Stan English. He was in the police station's inquiry office, not the CID office.

'Nick Rhea, Stan,' I introduced myself. 'I'm with CID at the moment and have been sent to a crime reported earlier today. Theft of cash from St Patrick's Church. I'm there now. The priest-in-charge knows nothing about this, so can you tell me who reported it?'

'It should be in the occurrence book, Nick. Give me half a minute.' I heard him place the phone on the desk while he searched. There was a rustling of paper and then he said, 'Yes, found it. Reported this morning at 8.40 a.m. by a Mr John Milner from a phone box. He gave his address as St Patrick's Church and rang off. We couldn't reconnect with him so we passed the details – not many, I'm afraid – to CID who said they would deal with it.'

'Thanks, Stan. I'll see what we make of this. I'm in St Patrick's presbytery with Monsignor O'Leary.' I rang off then relayed this information to the priest, asking, 'So does this make any sense?'

'To be honest, Nick, it doesn't. For one thing I've never heard of John Milner. So far as I know he's not a member of our congregation but in any case neither I nor Father John would report the theft of cash from that collection plate. It's there to be taken by anyone. We trust and pray that no one will abuse our generosity. We get beggars calling for financial help and others who are homeless or out of work and in need of temporary support due to a lack of funds so we place money there so they can take what they need when they need it without the embarrassment of begging or asking for help. In this way, they can get funds – small but important – without getting bogged down with formalities, permissions, questions about their current way of life and so on. It's a charity that cuts out all that red tape and political nonsense.'

'So when the plate's empty, you simply replenish it?'

'Yes, we do. We usually put in a handful of pound notes with coins to hold them down to stop the wind blowing them away when the doors are opened. I've personally had words with one of our regular travellers, a tramp called Rufus, to explain our system and he promised not to abuse it. He appreciates having a small fund available when he needs it, and he has passed details to his fellow travellers. Quite simply, Nick, there's always a few pounds in notes or cash on that plate and other churches do likewise. It's an unpublicized part of our charitable work.'

'And John Milner means nothing to you?'

'Sorry, no. But his actions have had one effect, Nick. He's alerted me to the fact the plate is empty and needs refilling!

Maybe that was his intention? I shall do so with no further ado.'

'And I shall have to find the right words to write this off as "no crime". Some of my long-term police officers will find it hard to believe that you place money on a plate for anyone to help themselves. But I can see the sense in this – some of us don't like to ask for charity, and I suspect some will repay their "loan" with interest!'

'So they do! I've known people put their own money into that plate, Nick, for others to make good use of. So what do you make of this mysterious John Milner?'

'All sorts of possibilities come to mind,' I told him. 'As you suggest, it might have been someone needing money and found none. Was it his way of getting the plate refilled for a return visit?'

'Quite possible. But he'd need coins for that phone call, Nick. It was hardly a case for a 999 call.'

'So did he visit the presbytery this morning?'

'Someone did but Miss Carey didn't get a good description except to say he looked like a tramp but said he had no time to wait around. I was celebrating Mass, you see, and Father John was helping out at the hospital, so we never saw the man. There was no sign of him when I finished Mass and the congregation had dispersed. Miss Carey said he hurried off immediately, but gave no reason for his wish to speak to the priest-in-charge.'

'So he would be able to ring the police from a kiosk at 8.40 a.m., which is when John Milner's call was timed?'

'I'd say so, yes.'

'So even if his message about no money in the kitty had reached you, there'd be nothing for him if he had returned immediately?'

'No, the plate would still be empty then. Does that matter?'

'Well, so far as I can see, he has not committed any crime because the money was there as a donation to whomever took it. We always need someone to lodge an official crime complaint. Without that, this investigation must be concluded.'

'With that, I would agree,' said the priest, smiling.

When I returned to the CID office, I explained this to DI Baldwin, who listened carefully, then said, 'You did the right thing, Nick. It's no crime, no detection and no arrest. You're still waiting for that … but it's one less crime on our books! And I'm not going to order one of my Ds to pretend to pray in church whilst watching that plate!'

CHAPTER 7

DESPITE NOT HAVING made an arrest, my early days as a D were proving interesting and productive, far busier than I had expected. When in uniform, I'd spent a lot of time just parading around or standing on street corners, observing the passing scene and theoretically preventing crime and keeping the peace. We waited for things to happen whereupon we would respond, but otherwise we did very little creative work. We might have been criticized for our inactivity but our mere presence in those distinctive uniforms was both a deterrent to offenders and reassuring to the public. Like an insurance policy, we were there when needed. Things were different now I was a keen young detective in the making. Every minute of my working day was occupied and for that I was thankful. Boredom was one thing I would not have to tolerate during my new duties.

'Take your refreshment break early,' suggested DI Baldwin as lunchtime approached one morning. 'Then I'll explain your new task.'

After my three-quarters of an hour break, when I went to my digs for a light lunch, DI Baldwin said, 'Nick, that task I promised, I think you'd better have some experienced help so I've asked Sherlock to join you. He's downstairs in the muster room checking some files – join him there and he'll explain things.'

Sherlock Watson was a thin-faced, unsmiling, hawk-nosed individual, about forty-five years old, and he had long service as a detective in Strensford. His name came about because his father, surnamed Watson, was an ardent fan of the Sherlock Holmes stories. Watson Senior must have been delighted when his son decided to join the police and become a real-life detective.

By way of keeping faith with his father's dream, Sherlock always wore tweed suits, plus-four trousers, brown brogue shoes, a deer-stalker hat and carried a magnifying glass in his pocket. A splendid meerschaum pipe was often hanging from his lips too. He played up to his image and I think some people honestly thought he was a descendant of the great detective, believing that the original Sherlock Holmes was a real person, not the product of a writer's imagination.

Apparently, however, our Sherlock was a good detective with an abundance of local knowledge because he had been born in the town, educated at the local grammar school, married a local lass and spent his entire working life in Strensford. Upon leaving school, he'd had a spell working in Strensford Co-op but found the work lacked interest, and so he had joined the police, initially patrolling in uniform and eventually becoming a detective.

I had no idea whether he had been transferred to CID because of his experience and skills, or whether the image he created had persuaded others he was a good detective. Whatever the background, however, I reasoned that Sherlock would add his knowledge and experience to our inquiries.

'Sit down, Nick,' he invited as he examined lots of papers spread across the large table in the muster room. 'This could be interesting.'

'So what's our task?'

'Someone broke into the Co-op during the night and has got away with thousands of cigarettes. Player's in packets of twenties, a hundred and twenty packets to a carton. That's two thousand, four hundred cigarettes to a carton, and five cartons have been taken, packed into one box – twelve thousand cigarettes! Fairly lightweight – it's an amount that could be carried by one person.'

'Was a vehicle involved?' I asked.

'Chummy wouldn't need a vehicle to get away with that load.'

I persisted. 'He must have had a car or some other vehicle waiting? Even a wheelbarrow. You couldn't walk unseen through the streets at night carrying a load like that even though cigarettes aren't very heavy! You've been to the scene, have you?'

'I have indeed; it brought back memories of my teenage years working there.'

'So what did you learn from that?' I pressed.

'Not a lot. Chummy smashed a ground-floor window in an office at the back, well out of sight and sound of the street and passers-by, climbed in and made his way to the stockroom, helped himself to the box of Player's and left via the back door, unlocking it and re-locking it by dropping the latch after he'd gone. Initial local inquiries suggest nobody heard a thing, and there are no fingerprints or other evidence. Just a gap where the cigs were stored.'

'Someone knew where to go and what to find?' I posed my comment as a question.

'Exactly,' agreed Sherlock. 'An inside job, perhaps? The total stolen in that raid is actually small bearing in mind the total stocks that are usually kept there. They'll sell quickly in the pubs or in back streets, at a discount, of course. Unless you worked there you'd hardly notice a carton was missing. Even so, the stockroom manager spotted it when he arrived for work at half seven this morning.'

'Is he sure it was taken overnight? Last night?' I asked.

'As sure as he can be, but he admitted he doesn't stock take every night before going home. There's a lot of movement in there during a working day.'

'That would be normal. So is there something about it in those papers?' I indicated the files open before him.

'I'm checking to see whether other Co-ops in this part of the world have recently had similar thefts or break-ins. As big stores go, the Co-op is regularly raided, more so than other stores of comparative size. Booze and fags are the main targets because they're easily disposed of. No questions asked in pubs and so on. And Co-op are lagging behind in security measures; they're far too old-fashioned and unimaginative even if they have reinforced their rear doors and windows, especially on the ground floor.'

'Has anything else caught your eye?' I asked hopefully. 'Anything that might be significant?'

'Just that over the last three years, thirty-two Co-ops have been attacked at night by break-ins, and in thirty of those cases, the targets were alcoholic drinks and cigarettes. In other cases, cosmetics, foodstuffs and children's clothing were taken. No one got away with a three-piece suite or an easy chair! As a result of earlier raids of this kind, some Co-ops have installed what are in effect giant safes to store liquor and cigarettes when not on open sale, but even one of those was raided in Liverpool and broken into with road drills. Alcohol was stolen. The greater the riches, the more temptation they present, and the more violent the execution of the raids. Fortunately, no member of staff has been hurt but some stores are now employing night-watchmen in the hope of reducing the crimes.'

'Do members of staff steal from the shop?'

'Inevitably, and some are caught by store detectives. Normally, violence is not used in those cases; they sneak the goods out when leaving work.'

'So is this Strensford Co-op's first raid of this kind?' I asked.

'It is, but it does regularly suffer from shoplifters – other than staff – despite a store detective being on the premises during opening hours. As an example, individual packets of cigarettes are stolen – easily slipped into a bag or pocket. That's a sadness in all shops where the stocks are temptingly within reach of both staff and customers – there are lots of dishonest people about!'

It was beginning to look as if I was superfluous to this inquiry but I knew I'd been sent mainly to gain experience. I got the feeling I was interrupting his thoughts. Clearly, most of the initial work had been done earlier – examination of the scene, tests for fingerprints and other evidence, interviewing of witnesses, checking stocks to ascertain whether other items had been stolen and so forth.

I knew the uniform branch would have been notified and they would be making inquiries around the town in the hope of either tracing the stolen goods or locating witnesses. There seemed little that I could contribute. But I was determined not to be shuffled into the sidings, as a manner of speaking. I still hadn't made that elusive first arrest as a D, and this crime might provide the opportunity.

'Would you object if I had a look at the scene?' I asked Sherlock.

'Why do you want to do that?' He frowned as he looked at me. 'We've done all that's necessary; it's now a case of tracing witnesses and asking questions in town in the hope of turning up a suspect or two. Or even tracing the stolen goods.'

'I'm aware of all that, Sherlock. It's just that I always feel it's necessary for an investigating officer to visit the crime scene.'

'Well, I can't argue with that, Nick, so yes, go along and ask the manager to show you where it all happened. I think you'll find we've covered everything that's necessary but I'll phone him to say you're on the way. His name is Frank Stoker.'

'Thanks.'

'Give him my compliments. You'll need some kind of proof that you're a CID man so don't forget your warrant card.'

When I arrived at the Co-op in Duke Street, I asked for Mr Stoker, adding that I was expected. I was shown to an upstairs office where I was escorted in and introduced to the manager, who rose to his feet from behind his desk.

'DC Rhea!' He smiled as my escort vanished. 'How can I help?'

He was a tall, grey-haired man in his late fifties, I estimated, smartly dressed in a dark grey suit. 'Please take a seat. How can I help? We had your officers here this morning.'

'So I'm led to believe. I joined the team rather late in the day and would like to look at the scene, if you could show me. My colleague, DC Watson, is aware of this.'

'To be honest, Mr Rhea, there is very little left of the debris – even the glass window has been repaired although we did wait for your officers to finish examining the scene before making good the damage. We need to act quickly if our damaged windows or doors give access to the premises. Anyway, we'll co-operate as well as we can and we hope your colleagues manage to trace the perpetrator. Now come with me.'

He led me down a rear staircase to the ground floor and through a maze of corridors until we reached an outer door. It opened into a small covered passage wide enough to accommodate a car or small van. At one end were full cycle racks while the other opened on to the street where the store's main entrance was located. It was a very useful side entrance, safe from the elements but open to trespassers.

'It was a pane in this door.' He opened the wooden door and showed me the new pane of glass with its putty not yet dry. 'He smashed it and reached through to unfasten the lock inside.

Once inside, he had the run of the building. There's no permanent night-watchman here, they're too expensive for a small store of this kind, although we will always consider drafting in one temporarily from one of our larger stores if we feel it is necessary.'

'And no street lights in this side entrance?'

'No, but we have several internal lights that burn all night, high enough in the ceilings to avoid being extinguished by unauthorized visitors!'

'But able to guide a thief to his loot at night?'

'Sadly, yes.'

'Did my colleagues remove the broken glass?'

'Yes, I had swept it up to avoid our staff getting punctures in their cycle tyres when they arrived at work so your scenes of crime officers took it away to be scientifically examined for fingerprints or anything else.'

'Burglars sometimes cut themselves when breaking glass,' I told him. 'Their blood provides good evidence. Now can I see where the loot was taken from?'

'Of course.'

He led me through several offices and corridors until we entered the stockroom. Its racks and shelves were full of varied boxes and crates of merchandise, and I could see a gap among the cigarettes.

'Here.' He patted the base of the gap. 'Twelve thousand cigarettes ... worth a good deal in cash over the counter of a pub or club with no questions asked. We're covered by insurance, of course, but we must establish that the goods were stolen and that it was not an internal crime by a member of staff, hence our report to the police.'

'Thanks, Mr Stoker, it's good of you to spare the time. Now if you could show me the way back to an exit, I'll let you get back to your work.'

*

It was a ten-minute walk back to the police station and when I looked in the muster room, DC Sherlock Watson was not there, nor was his file of papers. I therefore headed upstairs to the CID office. Detective Sergeant Latimer was in the office when I arrived and it was evident he knew what I had been doing.

'Any luck, Nick?'

'Yes,' I said with confidence.

'You'd better come into my office and tell me all about it; the others are all out, including your mate Sherlock. He's rushed off to Handale for a word with their Co-op manager.'

As I settled beside his desk, he invited me to recount my adventures. I provided him with a lot of detail, but added as my punchline: 'I'm sure it was an inside job, Sarge.'

'We've come to that conclusion but we need evidence, Nick. And there is none.'

'I think there is. First, no stranger entering at night could have found his way into that warehouse and back out again with a load. It's like a maze; a stranger would get lost.'

'Point taken, Nick, but that is not evidence, it's a theory.'

'I think it is supporting evidence, Sarge, but there is more.'

'I'm listening.'

'When the window of the rear entrance was smashed, the glass fell into the passage outside. That indicates it was broken from the *inside*.'

'How do you know that? My officers said the glass had been swept up …'

'It was swept up to avoid the staff puncturing their bike tyres, that's what the manager told me. That means the pieces fell outside and it suggests the window was smashed from the inside. By someone hiding on the premises, someone who knows their way around?'

'Well, we brought some pieces here this morning so we'll

give them a real good scientific examination. I'm impressed, Nick, but you've not come up with the name of a suspect.'

'One who rides a bike, perhaps, with panniers or a butcher's-style tray that would have carried those cigarettes away.'

'Now this is interesting, Nick. Sherlock rushed off to Handale Co-op because one of their staff was transferred to Strensford about a year ago. He came under a cloud at Handale – stuff was disappearing from the shelves but he was never caught – suspected but always able to convince his bosses that he was innocent. Sherlock is getting more background to this as we speak – but if that man is now working at our Strensford Co-op, then he's ripe for an interview first as a witness but probably as a suspect. Thanks for this, Nick. I'll see to this and will keep you informed.'

As I turned to leave, DS Latimer said, 'No arrest for this one, Nick, but I'm sure we'll find another case for you to deal with.'

CHAPTER 8

'IT'S A MATTER of very discreet observations on a shop, Nick.' DS Latimer was explaining my new commission. 'Sinclair's tobacconist and newsagent. You know it?'

'I do. It's just across the bridge on the left.'

'That's the one. Do you know anything about it? Or its owner? Did you pick up any gossip during your time in uniform? Or even when you were at school here?'

'I heard rumours at school,' I admitted. 'So is it being targeted by shoplifters?'

'That's the gist of things. What sort of rumours did you hear?'

'Kids leaving school in their dinner break and coming down town to steal sweets from Woolworths, make-up from the chemists and cigarettes from Sinclair's. They thought it was some kind of game.'

'Those kind of shops always attract shoplifters, Nick. Just ask the management of Woolworths! I know some who put displays on the counter with the deliberate intention of having the sweets stolen. They're old sweets, out of date but harmless. It's a fine way of clearing the shelves of old stock so we never received complaints about it. But that's not what I'm referring to.'

'Old Mr Sinclair's not been accused of indecency with

children, has he?'

'Why do you ask that?'

'It was well known in my school days – and that was only six or seven years ago – that girls were stealing packets of cigarettes and openly stuffing them down their knickers before leaving the shop. Mr Sinclair was helpless to do anything in case he got accused of assaulting the girls. He wrote to our headmaster and all the children were warned at assembly that the police had been informed.'

'That was before my time here, but it didn't stop?'

'No, the girls treated it as a joke and the lads joined in, nicking cigarettes and dodgy magazines from the top shelf.'

'Well, it's still going on, Nick, Jim Sinclair has made an official complaint about secondary schoolchildren stealing items from his shop. The way he told the tale made it sound like mass trespass and theft. A crowd of them enter the shop, some with satchels, and distract him while their mates – boys and girls – do the stealing. He's an old man now, Nick. If the school can't stop them, we need to teach them a hard lesson.'

'Wait outside and search them, you mean?'

'That's no good; they'd spot us outside waiting and would leave with empty hands, knickers or satchels, as innocent as newborn babes. We might even get into trouble for harassing them! So the first thing we need to do is identify the thieves along with the precise times of their visits – and we need to do so without them being alerted to our actions. You know the old saying – softly, softly, catchee monkey!'

'Yes, I've heard that. So what are you proposing?'

'For one thing, we need to establish their system – you know what I mean. A criminal committing the same crime in the same place at the same time each day – a pattern of events in other words. That's always good evidence of criminal intent; it would remove the defence that they'd taken the goods but forgotten to pay. Also we need to identify the culprits. I know the uniforms will identify their school but we need to put names to faces.'

'But we will need to catch them in possession of the stolen goods?' I added.

'That comes later, Nick. We need to watch them over a period to establish their guilt. Once we've done our preliminary work, we pounce! And catch them all in possession of goods they've not paid for. We'd have to take Jim into our confidence at some point, asking him to mark his packets of cigarettes in some way, or the other items regularly stolen like bars of chocolate or whatever.'

'And we'd need several plain clothes officers waiting outside the shop, mingling with the crowds to be anonymous, to stop and search them.'

'That also comes later, Nick. Our first task is to establish that Jim's shop is under regular attack from those kids – we need to find out if they come on a particular day of the week, a regular time, say, school dinner hour. We're seeking to establish a pattern before we launch our Operation Goodie!'

'A good name for it,' I added, the only comment I could think of at the time. 'So what's my function?'

'You're fairly new here, and when out of uniform you'll not be known to many people. I want you to pose as a tourist and take photographs of those kids entering the shop and leaving, with a note of their precise timings. That's the first thing for us – from that, we should be able to put names to faces, with a bit of help from the teaching staff, and from there we will build our case.'

'I've no claim to be a photographer, sir!'

'You don't need to be professional, just competent. We have good cameras, all official police issue with an ample stock of film. You're familiar with cameras, I trust?'

'I am, but with all due respect I won't be able to take photos inside his shop.'

'I'm not asking you to do that!'

'That's a relief!'

'I want you in the street outside, looking like a tourist. Don't make it obvious you're snapping the youngsters, pretend you're taking harbour scenes or shots of the old town. If anyone asks, tell them you're working as a freelance for a travel magazine or a newspaper who has commissioned a feature about the town and its harbour along with tourism and the fishing industry. It might get people talking to you – make the most of anything like that.'

'So do you want me to take pictures of all the children?'

'You'll have to be careful how you tackle this, Nick. We don't want reports of a snooper sneaking pictures of pretty young girls, we don't want you reported as a suspect paedophile, but you must take as many pics as you can without raising alarm. Use your own judgement, particularly as the kids enter and then emerge from the shop. We need to know how long they remain inside – so notes of times are vital. Photographers do that when taking pics for magazines. They note all the details. What we need is some idea of the scale of the problem so you might need to repeat your visits several times, even with new disguises if you think it necessary.'

'I'm sure the kids won't recognize me.'

'You can't be too sure but if they're chattering about the forthcoming raiding party, they might not notice you lurking under a Kiss Me Quick hat!'

'With the crowds of tourists we get here, even out of the holiday season, I should be able to lose myself among them. So what will happen to the photos?'

'We'll collate them in the office as we analyze the supporting evidence, then once we're sure of our ground, we'll ask the school to put names to faces. From there we can find out home addresses to interview the suspects in the presence of their parents. It's going to take a long time, Nick, but we can be very patient.'

'Do you mean I should accommodate it along with my other inquiries?'

'I do. It means you'll have a few busy lunchtimes as a tourist but the important thing is not to draw attention to yourself – don't hang around all day. Dash in, take your pics and leave to deal with other cases. A change of hat or other clothing, dark glasses, an ice cream in your hand and so on might persuade folks you're nothing more than an average camera-happy tourist. And one other thing – you are not alone in this, it's a team effort, so you'll get support from my officers and we'll inform Jim Sinclair of our plans, it will be our response to his report of the crimes. I believe he must be informed of our actions but we must persuade him to behave as normal, which might not be easy. In short, we need to catch these thieves red-handed and nip their crime careers in the bud. For their own sakes as well as Jim's.'

'I understand,' I said.

He handed me a smart Kodak in a shoulder holster plus several rolls of fast film, and, once satisfied I knew how to use it, said, 'Enjoy your role as a photographer recording the continuing harbour scene here in Strensford, Nick. Now to get you started, Shirley Robinson will be doing the same. You could appear to be a happy couple on holiday. Liaise with her.'

Shirley was one of the Strensford detectives who specialized in offences against women and children. Even though this case contained no suggestions that such crimes were being committed, I was sure her input would be valuable.

'Any questions, Nick?'

'Not at the moment, sir.'

'Right. As I said earlier, there's another matter that needs your attention. Are you tied up with anything urgent right now?'

'Not at the moment, sir.'

'It's a simple task. I've had a report from Sea View Guest House on West Cliff that a couple have disappeared without paying. If my memory serves me well, we got advance notice of these people in the Crime Information – they've been travelling around England and Wales always leaving their hotel or boarding house without paying.'

'Quite a regular occurrence in seaside resorts, I believe.'

'It is, and usually it's not our concern because it is classed as a civil debt, not a crime. But go along and find out what it's all about, Nick. Let's see if Strensford CID can nail these rogues. The owners of Sea View are a Mr and Mrs Townsend.'

Before leaving to undertake my two tasks, I went to the muster room downstairs to examine the file of daily Crime Information sheets in the hope of finding a description of the fraudsters. I found two cases, one in Saltburn-by-the-Sea and the other in Runswick Bay, both on the north-east coast of Yorkshire.

In each case, a man and woman, purporting to be man and wife, had stayed at a boarding house and left without paying. The hotels and boarding houses had their own telephoned early-warning system for alerting their colleagues to such people, but the names given at those two resorts were different.

The Saltburn couple called themselves Mr and Mrs T. Williams and the Runswick pair were Mr and Mrs W. Thomas. The descriptions were vaguely similar – the ages of the pair was given as between forty-five and fifty-five, the woman being younger than the man. He was average height and build with greying hair and she had long dark hair swept back, held in place with a red ribbon. They were described as very pleasant, ordinary people with no discernible accents, each casually dressed in holiday clothes but not scruffy.

Neither report indicated they had a car; they were thought to have arrived by the local bus service. There was no indication of their home district and there were no other factors that might identify them. The addresses they had written in those two boarding house registers before their arrival in Strensford had been checked and were found to be false. That would upgrade the incident to the status of a misdemeanour: credit by fraud.

I jotted down the salient details, made sure my camera was loaded with film, and left the police station on my twin missions. As the schools were still in session, my first stop was at Sea View Guest House perched high on the West Cliff. It was a white terraced house of four storeys and was instantly recognizable as a seaside boarding house. There was a notice on the door asking visitors to enter the hallway and ring the bell for attention, so I walked in.

Very helpful to me once inside was the formal hotel register; it was on a table in the entrance hall, open with a ballpoint conveniently placed. This register recorded the details of all who made use of the sleeping accommodation, with the visitors having to write their names, addresses, car registration numbers, nationality and next destination if applicable. Of course, there was no means of testing the truthfulness of such entries until inquiries arose, such as the one I was currently investigating.

By then, it was usually too late – the dishonest birds had flown. I glanced at the names of recent guests but did not find a Williams or a Thomas, so I rang the bell. A small woman with dyed blonde hair and of indeterminate middle age responded immediately.

'If it's for a single tonight, we can fit you in,' she said, smiling. 'Bed and board ten shillings and six per person per night, evening meal extra but you must order in advance. No lunches.'

'No thanks, I'm not looking for accommodation. I am Detective Constable Rhea.' I found my warrant card and showed it to her. 'I believe you rang about a couple who left without paying?'

'Yes, I did. I'm Beryl Townsend. You'd better come through to the lounge. A cup of tea, perhaps?'

'That would be most welcome.'

She called to someone in the kitchen to bring a tray of tea and biscuits into the lounge as we went through. I settled in an easy chair with my pocket book open, ready to take notes next to my descriptions of previous offenders.

'Tell me about them,' I invited.

'There's not much to tell.' She sighed. 'This couple arrived yesterday afternoon and asked for a double for one night with dinner and breakfast this morning. I agreed. They seemed a nice ordinary couple.'

'Man and wife?'

'Yes, they signed the register as Mr and Mrs D. Cummins from an address in Lancashire, and said they would pay cash on departure. When I waited for them to come down to breakfast, I realized it was getting late and checked their room. They'd gone, and neither me nor my husband heard a thing. I checked the Lancashire address through a friend over there – it was false. And they left no money in payment. Nothing.'

She could only provide a very sketchy description of the couple, which might have matched those I already had. Their accent, she told me, had a slight Cockney twang although it might have been a southern accent from Kent or somewhere else in the south-east. I told her about the other two local cases but it was impossible to be certain they were all the same people despite vague similarities in their appearance.

'Don't your experts come and take fingerprints in the room?'

she asked. 'There must be some way of stopping this kind of thing – it happens such a lot in our industry.'

'It's not classed as a serious crime, Mrs Townsend. In fact, some police forces regard these incidents as a civil debt, not a crime, and to categorize it as a crime there needs to be evidence of fraud. If fraud can be proved, perhaps a false address, then we could prosecute them summarily in the magistrates' court, but the hard part is identifying them, catching them and then proving the fraud.'

'Crooks like that must not get away with it! We trusted them.'

'We'll do our best to trace them. We'll circulate details as far as we can, but you might find it better to get a cash payment in advance or take a deposit. And remember cheques can bounce.'

'Don't I know it! There are times, Mr Rhea, when I think everyone out there in the big wide world is a crook!'

'I think you might consider some kind of mutual aid scheme where hoteliers and guest house keepers pass details of their experiences to, say, ten contacts who in turn send it to a further ten ad infinitum. You'd need good descriptions and as much detail as you could muster with car numbers if they travel by car. It might prove to be a useful early-warning system if these characters are touring the coast, obtaining free accommodation and food along the way. It does happen!'

'We have a system already but it's a bit hit and miss. We never know where these rogues are going to stay next.'

'We'll circulate details in our own publications but to catch and stop these rogues means a big effort from you and your colleagues. And perhaps some form of security upon their arrival. I knew one hotelier who always asked male customers to leave their watches in the hotel safe until departure. They didn't like it, but it worked. Basically, though, non-payment of a bill is not a criminal offence – and so the police are powerless to investigate. But as I said earlier, if fraud is involved it changes things and we can then make inquiries. In your case, there was fraud.'

'Thanks, Mr Rhea, you've set me thinking. I might contact other guest house keepers in town, or further afield, and we'll see what we can do if we work together.'

Having done all that I could, it was now time to pose as a tourist with a camera.

CHAPTER 9

As I WALKED along Strensford's main street towards Sinclair's shop, I passed the old town hall, an atmospheric building where many important events occurred. These ranged from civic functions to weddings, all of which attracted photographers, and I found myself wondering how I could make myself less conspicuous as I carried out my photographic assignment. Somehow, it was necessary for me to become invisible as I photographed those schoolchildren.

As I strode past, I could not avoid recalling one earnest constable in uniform who was ordered by his shift sergeant to go home and put on a civilian jacket as there were some covert observations that urgently demanded his attention. Off went the constable, who returned shortly wearing a civilian jacket. But he had not changed his uniform trousers, shirt, tie and boots; I must admit, I was surprised he had left his peaked cap at home. (We did not wear helmets – we wore peaked caps that made us look like bus conductors or postmen.) In fact, one day when I was patrolling in uniform, a tourist asked whether I was a postman or a policeman. Thinking he was joking, I said I was a hotel commissionaire.

It is true that some older constables, probably having served in the army, obeyed commands to the letter – we called them uniform carriers and they were quite good at standing on street corners looking fierce, but if they were told to undertake any specific task that required tact, discretion or initiative, it had to be very carefully explained.

One of the memories resurrected now involved such an individual. He was ordered by his sergeant to patrol Bakersgate, the street which contained the town hall, and prevent all vehicles from parking between 9 a.m. and 11.30 a.m.

The reason was that the county's Lord Lieutenant was coming at 10.30 to formally open an exhibition of original drawings, paintings and sculptures that depicted Strensford over the years. The occasion was the tercentenary of the town hall and it was to be attended by the county's civic leaders, Members of Parliament and other dignitaries. Members of the press were expected too. All this was explained to the constable; I was one of the uniformed constables who had to stand guard at the main door to salute the official party as they arrived.

But when the small motorcade with the Lord Lieutenant's flag-flying car in second place behind an unmarked police car entered the street, with a couple of press cars following, the worthy constable waved them forward and ordered them not to park in the street. They all disappeared, only to return a few minutes later, to be once again directed away. They did not return a third time.

Then the duty sergeant turned up – on foot.

'Have they all gone in?' he asked the worthy constable, who was still patrolling the empty street.

'Who? And where, Sergeant?'

'The Lord Lieutenant and his party.' The sergeant by now no doubt had a sinking feeling in the pit of his stomach. 'Don't tell me …'

'I saw that smart car and a procession behind it so I waved them through, Sergeant. And I stopped everybody from parking as you had ordered. I made sure the visitors had a clear run.'

'I expected you to use your initiative!'

'You never told me to.'

'It was the official party you waved through, Constable, so where will they be?'

'In the public car park, I expect, Sergeant, where all cars should park.'

And so it transpired. The official party had found spaces in the public car park just behind Bakersgate and they all appeared on foot in a small procession. The Lord Lieutenant hailed the sergeant.

'A problem, Sergeant?' he asked.

'Yes, sir, a smell of gas. We thought we'd better keep the street clear of traffic until the emergency services located the cause.'

'Well done! The job must go on, Sergeant!'

And so the event took place with a headline in the local paper the following Friday that announced, 'Emergency alert in town', which also praised the quick thinking of the town sergeant in averting a disaster following a leakage of gas. The gas company denied all knowledge of such a leak.

I decided to stand near the end of the harbour bridge with my camera at the ready. Despite being dressed in a light shirt and slacks with a camera slung around my neck, I felt very conspicuous. As the weather was mild and warm, I had left my jacket in the CID offices, confident it would not be required. In spite of my attempts to appear casual, I felt just like a police officer in disguise who was trying to look nothing like a police officer.

All I had to do was look like a tourist and take some photographs. I pretended to be assessing the touristy scenes around me, pointing the camera and checking the light. By this stage of the day, it was dinner time at the town's schools. Suddenly the street corner was busy with children, boys and girls in school uniform, heading for Sinclair's shop. I noticed all were carrying satchels. There were a dozen at least.

I found a wonderful vantage point in a disused doorway which overlooked the shop's entrance, from where it looked as if I was taking photographs of the townscape. The steeples of many ancient churches were prominent and some of the loftier terraces were bathed in the light of the midday sunshine. I decided I could spend some time here, surreptitiously snapping youngsters as they both entered and left the shop. And so I did, making sure I caught their faces and any other distinctive features. One boy I noticed wore white plimsolls with his navy blazer and long grey trousers. I wondered if he had seafarers in the family as I got a good shot of him.

I used three reels of film but felt I had succeeded in capturing what I hoped were realistic images; that their identities should be easily achieved by their class teachers. I decided not to overdo the time I spent there and so I made a discreet exit. I would return another day. One thing I did notice was that the children were all laughing and joking as if this was some sport or game. My initial part in this investigation was over and I felt sure my efforts were good enough to prove the crimes, and thus prevent any more.

The walk back to the police station would take about quarter of an hour and I decided to take the shortest route along Bakersgate, then via Duke Road and up the cobbled hill to the old building which, more than a century earlier, had been converted into our police station. With the town hall standing proud, Bakersgate was regarded as the main street of Strensford but it was very narrow, with the first floors of the older buildings projecting into the street, having been built like that to provide shelter in stormy times centuries earlier. I'd seen similar street scenes in York's medieval thoroughfares and also in Chester.

Bakersgate was a thriving commercial centre and when I had served there as a uniformed police constable, the street was constantly busy, so much so that it had been subjected to a one-way traffic system with parking restrictions. Quite simply, the old street was too narrow for two vehicles, especially delivery lorries and buses, to safely pass one another or to avoid damaging the buildings. None the less, this remained the main shopping centre with high-street names like Marks & Spencer, Boots, Barclays Bank, Midland Bank and the post office all there. There were shoe shops, ladies' clothes shops, cafés, a couple of inns, bakeries and a range of other ventures including a dentist, photographic studio and a church patronized by an obscure Christian sect.

As I strode along the pavement, the door of one of the inns, the White Lion, burst open and two figures, apparently locked in mortal combat, hurtled into the street and fell over onto the pavement in a writhing heap directly in front of me. As one tried to get up – a large woman – the other made a great show of not allowing that to happen, along with much shouting, cursing, kicking of feet and waving of fists.

Then I recognized the big man. It was Claude Jeremiah Greengrass, whom I'd met earlier. He looked up at me hovering nearby and said, 'Constable Rhea, if I'm not mistaken. We can't go on meeting like this ...'

The figure beneath him was trying to shout but Greengrass prevented any sounds emerging by clapping his hand over her mouth. I must admit I was unsure what to do next, particularly as a small crowd was already gathering to enjoy the spectacle. As I was not in uniform, I felt I lacked authority.

'Claude Jeremiah Greengrass, if I'm not mistaken,' I began. I felt like saying, 'Hello, hello, hello, what's going on here?' but resisted, replacing it with, 'Well, Mr Greengrass, are you going to tell me what's happening?'

'I never talk to coppers if I can help it,' he muttered, struggling to his feet but keeping a firm grip on the woman's arm.

'Until now?' I ventured.

'This could be an exception. I've caught this old strumpet nicking money from that pub and when I tried to stop her she tried to run off so I went after her … but now I think it's a fella dressed up as a woman … he or she's certainly tough enough.'

By now the other was on her feet, looking distraught and unkempt. I thought it was a woman, albeit of a considerable size.

I asked, 'So did you steal money from this gentleman?'

'Gentleman!' she snorted. 'He's no gentleman, fighting with me like that … and I am not a man dressed as a woman! I am the mother of six children and grandmother to a further five.'

'Right.' I tried to take control of the situation before an ever-increasing audience. 'I am a police officer, Detective Constable Rhea, and it seems to me the pair of you might have to accompany me to the police station to sort out this matter.'

'I'm not having that!' began Claude. 'I'm innocent.'

'I did not steal any money!' shouted the woman and she delved somewhere into her mass of clothing and hauled out a collecting tin marked 'Lifeboat'.

'She did!' snapped Claude. 'I'd just dropped a couple of bob into that tin and she came into the bar and with not so much as a by your leave whipped the box from right under my nose and ran off with it.'

'I thought you were going to steal it!' she countered. 'You looked like a shady sort of character to me!'

'And so you had a good reason for protecting the tin?' I asked.

'Yes, I had. My name is Laura Goodwin and I am an authorized collector of these collection boxes. The landlady knows me well. I'm going around the town today, emptying them, counting the contents and issuing receipts to those who have kindly allowed us to display the tins.'

And as if to emphasize her role, she delved somewhere into her clothes and hauled out a leather bag which was fastened to a belt with a chain, and showed me her authorization card which was fixed to the bag. She rattled the bag to show it was heavy with cash. As the crowd increased, some of them cheered and the landlady of the White Lion then joined the fray to confirm Laura Goodwin's story.

'And,' she added dourly, 'we were not drinking after closing time. We were having a business meeting.'

'Right!' I shouted so that I could be heard. 'Clearly, there's been some misunderstanding and Mrs Goodwin was anxious to protect the donations for the lifeboat. Claude thought she was stealing the box and did his best to protect the cash. A good story all around. So I suggest Mrs Goodwin passes the box around you all so you can drop some loose change in to show gratitude for this free entertainment.'

There was a ripple of applause as the cash box circulated among the crowd, who were now dispersing rapidly.

Mrs Goodwin then apologized to Claude and he did likewise to her.

'Constable Rhea,' said Claude as we set about going our separate ways, 'I am not one for making friends with the constabulary or even talking to them on a friendly basis, but I thought you dealt with that affair very professionally. I am from the small village of Aidensfield up there on the moors, and I happen to know our local constable is nearing his retirement. If you're interested in a nice rural beat of your own in the future with some lovely people to deal with, I'll put in a good word for you. I'm told that your boss Blaketon is being sent to Ashfordly, which is nearby and gives him a station of his own to run. I reckon you'd make a good team.'

'I'm a bit young for that kind of responsibility just now,

Claude, but thanks. Who knows what the future will bring?'

'Who indeed? See you,' said Claude as he ambled away in his old dark brown overcoat.

I continued my walk to the police station with the first batch of photographs. As I made my way through the crowds, as anonymous as a police officer could be, I realized my first arrest in my new role as detective had almost been Claude Jeremiah Greengrass.

Making an arrest was not as simple as some might think. One important factor was that not all crimes and offences carried a power of arrest and so we had to be sufficiently versed in our craft to know when we could or should use our power of arrest. Another vital factor was that, before making an arrest, we should have sufficient evidence to justify it. Then we must be able to compile a crime report accompanied by witness statements that confirmed a crime had been committed whilst providing evidence of the guilt of the arrested person. Also, the proof would eventually be presented to a court of law where it would be contested by the defence counsel. In short, there was much to learn about the art of detecting crimes, tracing suspects, recording facts and arresting people.

I reached my destination. I labelled my films with the date and subject matter, then placed them in the tray used for transporting them to the photographic department for developing and printing. At that point I heard Detective Sergeant Latimer's voice.

'All OK, Nick?' he called from his office. He must have recognized the sound of my footfall or even the fact I had placed the films in the required place. I went through to speak to him and explain the events of my day, then he said, 'We need you tonight. Another observation job but without a camera. I'll explain things later.'

CHAPTER 10

'THE COTTAGE BELONGS to an MP,' DS Latimer explained. 'A Labour member who likes to come here anonymously. As a keen socialist, he doesn't want to be seen as a two-house owner, so he calls himself Dyer when he's here with his wife – Ken and Deidre Dyer – and he tells the local folk he works as a fitter for the Gas Board in Sheffield, which in fact he once did. We're aware of his real identity due to a measure of security surrounding his work – he is very ambitious and it is claimed he might one day be prime minister.'

'Clearly he likes wealth and power but daren't reveal his secrets to his constituents?' I put in for good measure.

'He's no different from a lot of Labour politicians, Nick, but his address in town is far from posh. It's 2 Stanton Yard, one of those narrow alleys that lead down to the harbourside from Harbour Heights. The cottages were once fishermen's homes but most are now holiday cottages, all very small with no garages. That causes difficulties especially when visitors park in the streets. Many of the fishermen who would have lived here in times past are now in either council houses or their own properties. Some did well and earned good money by owning their fishing boats. And you'll know as well as me that there are good herring seasons and bad ones.'

'All I know is that it's a mighty hard life, Sergeant.'

'Very.' He nodded. 'Not my cup of tea. I'd get seasick anyway! Now these cottages are in various stages of repair and upkeep. Some are deserted and almost derelict, no doubt awaiting somebody with money to buy them and do them up. A number have been modernized with bathrooms, water closets, modern sewage systems and electricity but a lot remain as they were in centuries past with earth toilets, no hot water and in some cases no electricity.'

'There are lots like that on the moors around here.'

'Those are usually in pretty rural locations. These occupy both sides of a narrow alleyway, each almost looking into the windows of the one opposite. The Dyers' is a neat modernized little house and Ken spends a lot of time here; it's his bolthole and on occasions he lets it to holidaymakers whom he knows well. Friends and family as a rule. His home town is Sheffield, but he's MP for Hunsford-on-Trent. His real name is Alfred Smith-Brown.'

He paused as I scribbled this information in my official notebook. When I indicated that I had it all recorded, he continued. 'The problem is that someone seems to have realized who he is, so he has alerted us to the fact his cottage might be a target for vandals or worse. He wants us to keep an eye on it.'

'Obviously he's got reasons for thinking this?'

'He has. He believes his cottage has been targeted in the past and is worried that it might be seriously damaged during his absences. We must take his claims seriously because of his increasing eminence in the political world.'

'So inquiries have already been made?'

'They have and we've kept observations from the house and also from properties standing opposite. We've learned nothing from those efforts but we must maintain our observations. Although we've never found any damage or vandals, he remains insistent that someone is out to harm him or his cottage. In his position, we can't ignore him.'

I felt I had to make a point here. 'Labour politicians are not very popular in this neck of the woods. I wouldn't be surprised if someone's recognized him and had a go at him.'

'My feelings too. I might add he upset herring fishermen around the country when he stood up in the Commons and proposed a quota for every North Sea fishing boat or trawler whether British or foreign. Our local fishing fleet owners were far from pleased by his attitude.'

'That suggests someone living *locally* has recognized him and has had a go at his property?' I offered.

'Exactly. And that's why we shall be keeping a close watch on his cottage by occupying it from time to time, not every night or day, but on irregular occasions so our movements don't attract undue attention. Softy, softly ... that's our plan, and now it's your turn.'

'So what do I do?'

'You'd better stay all night, there's food and drink in the pantry if you need more. All you have to do is maintain a watching brief overnight.'

'And remain awake?'

'Not necessarily but it'll mean going to bed late to catch any troublesome home-goers from local pubs and it'll be necessary to remain alert even when you're in bed. He says the noise is awful despite there being no outward sign of damage. We don't know what the vandals are doing, unless they're banging pans and kettles to keep him awake! But in any case make the house look occupied – lights on, crockery on the kitchen table, lounge curtains closed and so on. Leave the front bedroom window curtains open so you can get a good view of the alley if necessary.'

'So if someone is targeting Mr Smith-Brown's house for

whatever reason, I need to catch him in the act.'

'Difficult, but not impossible. I know it all sounds rather vague and we've not got a lot to go on, but we can't ignore this, Nick. He has registered a strong complaint and we can't take sides in politics. As always, the police must remain impartial.'

'I follow. Will I have any means of contacting the office quickly if something does occur?'

'There's a telephone in the house but no extension upstairs. You can use that to ring if you need assistance. Familiarize yourself with all aspects of the house just as you would if you were using it as a holiday cottage.'

'Right. So will you or anyone else be working late in CID?'

'No, not overnight. The uniform patrols are aware of this, by the way, and although they will be paying some passing attention to the house, they will not make it obvious that they are keeping it and its approaches under surveillance.'

'Good, that's helpful. I'm sure I can cope.'

'You can, and a lot depends upon the initiative of the officer who is attending the house at the time. You, in this instance.'

'I follow.' I hoped my brief response did not reveal my nervousness.

'Good, well, here's a set of keys.' He passed a small bunch to me. 'Doors back and front, there's window locks too, and some of the wardrobes and kitchen units have locks. It's because the house is used as a holiday cottage by various people who are not always family. If you could start at nine tonight while it's still light, it would help to make our presence seem normal. Leave in the morning when you're ready and report back to CID, say by nine o'clock. Now, any questions?'

'Have any of our observations produced a result?'

'No, nothing.'

'And is Mr Smith-Brown putting pressure on us to get a result?'

'He does write strong letters to the chief constable from time to time, asking if we have any news about his house, and whether we are continuing with our surveillance. And the chief then asks our superintendent ... so yes, there is pressure from high places – or from one rather high sort of place!'

We parted with DS Latimer wishing me the best of luck and an undisturbed night.

Later that night, I made my way to the cottage, approaching it from the harbourside and panting from the steep climb up the cobbled alley known locally as a yard. I passed several occupied cottages en route but noted that a lot were empty; indeed, several were ruinous. Number 2, my destination, was near the top and when I arrived I realized there was no number 1 – that site was an empty space with little sign of a house previously occupying it. All that remained was a concrete square with the alley's cobbles on one side and number 2 cottage on the other. The rear of number 2 backed onto a steep hillside overgrown with briars and weeds, while the top side opened into a narrow street with modern houses along its length. It did not climb the hillside like these yards; it was horizontal while overlooking the harbour. I realized that Mr Smith-Brown's house was the first that would be encountered by anyone entering Stanton Yard from the top. His cottage could be attacked and the culprits disappear into the darkness before anyone could react. I must admit I wondered if the 'attacks' were nothing but loud noises to aggravate Mr Dyer and prevent him from sleeping.

However, the attacks, whatever form they took, had to be from the front; there was no back door and the rear faced that mass of briars and weeds which was growing upon the cliff face.

There was no way anyone could approach the house from that direction. Somehow, the cottages had been built in a perilous location which seemed to have withstood the test of time despite the cliff's almost sheer gradient.

My first job was to examine the exterior to see whether there were any recent signs of damage or of anyone trying to break in, but I found nothing, not even old signs of damage to the door or windows.

I took a brief walk in the alley and other accessible areas to familiarize myself with the cottage and its environs, then let myself in via the Yale lock. There was no porch either outside or inside and the door opened directly into a tiny sitting room whose solitary window overlooked the alley. It was sparsely furnished with a two-seater settee and two cheap armchairs; there was no television set but one wall was occupied by a large radiogram and a cabinet for holding records. A few harbour-side prints graced the plain grey walls and a multi-coloured cheap square carpet covered most of the wooden floor. There was an open fireplace and a full scuttle of coal. A staircase led up from one corner with a cupboard under the stairs in which I found cleaning materials and a vacuum cleaner. A door in the rear wall opened into a small kitchen with views across the harbour; it contained the usual kettle, teapot, pots and pans, along with some tinned food on a cool shelf. The outer kitchen door led onto a tiny fenced balcony that accommodated the dustbin. Presumably its removal in readiness for the dustmen could only be accomplished by carrying it through the living room.

Upstairs were two bedrooms and a bathroom/toilet.

The double room was very small and only just managed to accommodate a bed, dressing table and wardrobe. It looked over the alleyway. The other bedroom, a single, was tiny with a bed tight against one wall and a tiny wardrobe along another with views over the harbour. The bathroom had a small bath and toilet with a frosted window overlooking the rear.

I had never been in such a tiny house but it was probably

ideal for holidaymakers who came only to sleep and eat here, spending most of their time outdoors. As DS Latimer had instructed, I would sleep – or lie awake – in the front bedroom with the curtains open so that I could look into the alleyway should anything happen. But I would put the light on in the rear bedroom and close the curtains to give an impression of someone sleeping there, away from the sounds and sights of the alleyway. Before going to bed I spent time in the lounge with the lights on and the curtains closed as I listened to the radio news, and some records from a surprisingly wide selection. Later, I went to bed armed with a torch.

I could not sleep. I had left the front bedroom window partially open, as well as the internal doors, so that I could hear any sound that might arise, voices or footsteps. But there was nothing. The alley was completely silent. No voices, no one chattering to friends in the alley, no one singing to themselves after a good night in a nearby pub. No traffic noises. Nothing. Not even seagulls squawking!

As I lay on the bed, I kept my slacks and shirt on just in case I had to rush outside and I made sure I knew where to lay my hands on the torch in the darkness. I lay on top of the sheets, but beneath the eiderdown. I heard a distant church clock strike the hours and must have dozed off at some point.

Then I was suddenly roused by the most alarming loud banging noises. I was dreaming about someone knocking me up and shouting that I was late for early-turn duty, then realized I was in a strange house supposedly wide awake to listen for these very noises.

I sat up in bed, shaking a little as the noises faded into nothingness. I wondered if it had all been a bad dream. I looked at my watch, luminous in the darkness, and it showed 1.15. Quarter past one in the morning. Not very late by some standards but the pub goers should be home by now.

As my sense of duty began to reassert itself, I knew I must get out of bed and make a search of the premises and outside. Relying on my torch, I found my way downstairs and into the lounge, but from the inside the windows looked secure. No broken glass, no mangled woodwork. I checked all the downstairs windows and none had been damaged. From the outside, there was no damage to the woodwork or stonework. I also checked the windows and doors of the adjoining cottages and those opposite but found absolutely no evidence of vandalism.

But there was no disputing that noise; it had been real enough and it had sounded like a man hammering something hollow near the cottages – I ruled out a musician practising drumming! Then I heard footsteps and a voice called out, 'All right, mate?'

'I thought I heard a banging noise,' I said as a middle-aged man appeared in the light of my torch.

He was heading up the alley and I thought I recognized him. 'I'm checking windows and doors.'

'You a cop then?'

'I am, a detective,' I answered.

'I'm just coming off shift at the bridge house,' he told me. 'Stan Middleton. We get your chaps in for a coffee sometimes ...'

'We've met there, Stan, when I was on uniform patrol. Now I'm on detective training, looking out for somebody who's thought to be trying to break into these cottages. There was a lot of banging.' I could see he was smiling as I went on, 'Like somebody thumping an empty oil drum with a sledgehammer.'

'That's a pretty good description. I heard it myself not two minutes ago, further down from here though.'

'So it's not an attempted burglary or act of malicious damage?'

'Nowt of t'sort.' He smiled. 'It happens from time to time and we think it comes from the Ocean Hotel on the cliff top.

When I say we, I mean those of us who work night shifts in town and have heard it – me, ambulancemen, firemen and so on. A plumber told us what it was.'

'So what is it?'

'Well, this plumber reckons you can't make it happen because it relies on pure chance circumstances in that hotel. If two particular toilets are flushed at exactly the same time on the first floor, and bath taps are turned off at precisely that moment on an upper floor, then you get a hammering noise which echoes down all the pipes leading from that hotel, and linking up with some drains in this part of town. There you are, young man. Your inquiries are complete.'

'Can it be proved?' I asked.

'Only by reproducing all those three causes at precisely the same moment. The din only lasts half a minute or so – no time to get there to see it or hear it happening. It takes a plumber to know that sort of thing!'

'Well, Stan, I owe you a great debt of gratitude.'

'Not me, it was that plumber who told us what it might be, it's him you should be thanking. If only I could remember his name ...' And off he went home.

I went back to bed and slept soundly until half past seven when the town came back to life. I got up, tidied the house and went to report for duty in the CID offices. DS Latimer was there.

'Well, Nick, did you sleep well or did you get that business sorted for us?'

'I did, Sergeant. In simple terms, Mr Smith-Brown would be better complaining to a plumber,' and I explained what I had learned.

He listened with a smile on his face. 'Thanks, Nick. I'll record these incidents as "no crime" and will recommend that Mr Smith-Brown wears earplugs when he stays here next.'

CHAPTER 11

NEXT MORNING, DETECTIVE Inspector Baldwin came into the CID office while I was talking to DS Latimer. 'Well done for sorting out the problem of the MP's plumbing noises. So how's the sleuthing going?'

'I'm enjoying it, sir. Very varied, busy and full of interest. There's always something to do.'

'Better than standing on street corners or plodding the streets looking out for parking offenders and drunken yobs?'

'Much better!'

'So you've not made an arrest yet?'

'Not yet, but I've learned a lot about keeping observations and asking questions.'

'Well, your time will come and meanwhile I've got a good one here.' Baldwin waved some sheets of paper he was carrying. 'You can accompany DC Rocky Salt on an inquiry on behalf of another force – Leeds City Police. Rocky?'

'Sir.' Detective Constable Peter 'Rocky' Salt rose from his work at the central table and joined us. He looked massive beside the DI, tall and broad with a boxer's flattened nose.

'This one's for you, Rocky. Take Nick along with you. It's a phoned request from Leeds City Police to trace, interview and eliminate – TIE as we call it, Nick. It involves a thug called

Pat The Bloody Butter who reckons he witnessed a murder in Roundhay Park in Leeds.'

'Recently?' asked Rocky. 'I had no idea that Pat The Butter strayed as far as Leeds.'

'Well, for one reason or another, it seems he was there, in Roundhay Park.'

'Doing what?'

'You tell me! It's one of the biggest parks in Europe so he had plenty of space to get into bother. Apparently, a man was knocked down and repeatedly kicked in the head by a gang of yobbos. The Butter reckons he saw it happen. He said the yobbos stole the victim's wallet and ran off. Other witnesses say The Butter was the sole assailant who ran off when a park attendant appeared on the scene.'

Baldwin passed the file to Peter Salt. 'That's something for you to sort out, Rocky. It's all in here. We know The Butter is a local tearaway and he's got plenty of form for violence. Butting people is one of his specialities, as you might have guessed by his nickname. Do what you can and if you think The Butter needs to be investigated as a suspect rather than a witness, bring him in. It might be an arrest for Nick – most young coppers want to arrest a murderer.'

'Right, sir.'

'Take the car, you might need it.'

Before leaving, Salt asked me to find Pat The Butter's file in our CID records. We wanted to know more about him before we confronted him and Salt told me the fellow's real name was Arvin Jones, a Welshman who worked in the shipyard who was a very good rugby player. In his early thirties, The Butter's huge size and enormous power could propel him through most man-made barriers and he regularly butted players from opposing teams. When he was off the rugger field and out with his mates, he usually drank too much and became aggressive. He'd head-butt anyone who annoyed him.

Quickly, I read a summary of his antics – The Butter seemed a character and a half, something you'd find in a comic or a film. But this man was real.

'You can see why we go double-handed to interview him; he can get quite rough at times,' said Peter as we headed for the CID car, a grey two-door Ford Anglia that lacked any suggestion it was a police car, except for the tell-tale aerial protruding from the boot. It was fitted with a police radio, a useful asset on occasions.

During our short journey of about a mile and a half to a huge council estate on the outskirts, Peter explained that Jones had a record of petty crime and convictions for several acts of violence that mainly consisted of fights outside clubs and pubs where he had knocked adversaries unconscious – but then he would steal any cash in his victim's pockets and make a dash for freedom. He was invariably affected by drinking too much beer before such occasions; when sober, he could be charming and polite, although still a terrifying sight for small people. And, we were led to believe, he was a very good workman at the local shipyard where boat-building of small craft and repairs were carried out. Arvin was a skilled carpenter.

It was not normal for us to interview suspects at their places of work but Leeds City Police had indicated there was an element of urgency about this inquiry, and it had been suggested we treat it as the interview of a witness rather than the questioning of a suspect. That should not make The Butter's bosses too antagonistic. DC Salt, who was himself a giant figure who played rugby and did a spot of wrestling in his spare time, had no qualms about meeting and interviewing The Butter.

I suspected that The Butter would also be well acquainted with Rocky, and that we would not generate a fight or wrestling match on this occasion. After parking in the visitors' car park, we reported to reception.

'Detectives Salt and Rhea from Strensford Police Station,' said Peter, showing the receptionist his warrant card. I did likewise.

'How can I help?' she asked.

'We'd like to have a few words with one of your workmen,' Peter explained. 'A man called Arvin Jones.'

'We don't normally allow our workforce to be interrupted during their working hours.' She did not smile. 'I'll have to ask the manager. Please take a seat.' She indicated two chairs in a waiting area.

She used an internal telephone to call the manager, who said he would come to speak with us. We waited. I guessed he would be checking his rule book about such requests. Then a slender man in a smart grey suit appeared at the counter, so we rose and joined him. He wore a badge that said, 'Ewan Mortimer. Shipyard Manager.'

'I cannot allow members of staff to be interviewed during working hours.' He did not smile either. 'I shall be pleased if you could arrange to speak with Mr Jones in his own time after work and not on these premises.'

'This is urgent.' Peter Salt stood his ground. 'It results from a request by Leeds City Police who believe your employee may have witnessed a serious assault in Roundhay Park. If he did not witness this incident then our chat will be finished within seconds. A simple no will suffice. If he *is* a witness, however, we may take a little while to obtain a written statement, which is vital if we are to arrest the suspect. I hope you will not interfere with the judicial processes, Mr Mortimer.'

'We have our procedures ...'

'So have we.'

There was a long pause as the little man struggled with his decision then he said, 'Well, I suppose this is an unusual exception to the rules. If you wait in the boardroom behind you, I shall ask Mr Jones to join you. Perhaps you will not detain him longer than necessary?'

'Of course not.'

And off he went.

We crossed the corridor to the room he had indicated and went in to find a long table with place settings ready for a dozen delegates. The walls were adorned with photographs and paintings of ships built on these premises, and there was also a rogues' gallery of eminent chairmen and directors who had steered the company through many years of successful production. We sat opposite one another at one end, leaving the end seat for The Butter – if he agreed to speak to us!

And so we waited. And waited.

After some twenty minutes, Peter developed a look of anxiety on his face, saying, 'We should have gone with that manager. I hope The Butter hasn't done a runner. Company rules have a lot to answer for ...'

He checked his watch.

'We've been here more than twenty minutes. That must be enough time to get him here from wherever he was working.'

Now we were faced with a dilemma.

'Wait here, Nick,' he said after another long pause. 'I'm going to see what's happening. I bet the manager has told him the cops wanted words and that could be enough to send him into escape mode.'

'That's a bit stupid,' I commented. 'He's only making things worse.'

'Not if he's guilty of that murder. If he turns up while I'm away, make sure he stays here. Chat him up with the witness line till I get back.'

And then he was gone, leaving the door open, and I was alone. As I wandered up and down the room, the receptionist came in.

'Mr Mortimer apologizes for the delay but he will return as soon as possible. He asked me to say that Mr Jones is not at his usual station and he is seeking him. He will inform you when there is any more news.'

'Did he mention my colleague?' I asked.

'No, where is he?'

'He's gone to look for your Mr Mortimer and our Mr Jones.'

'He is not allowed on the site unaccompanied,' she told me sternly. 'The management is very firm about that.'

'Then I'll stay here.' I smiled. 'I'd better not go out and get lost, or get myself into trouble.'

She produced a very weak smile and returned to her own office. Meanwhile, I had no idea where Rocky had gone or whether Mr Mortimer knew Rocky had attempted his own search for the elusive Mr Jones. The answer came after a further twenty minutes.

Peter returned with a dejected look on his large face, sat down opposite me and sighed. 'Gone, Nick. Disappeared into thin air. And none of his mates know where he is – or they're not telling.'

'Did Mortimer tip him off?'

'It seems not. His mates thought he had recognized the CID car in the car park and disappeared from his workbench.'

'Do we have his home address?'

'That's our next port of call, in a manner of speaking. He's unmarried and lives with his mother. I might add he has not got permission to leave work early, neither has he reported sick.'

As we discussed our next tactics, Mr Mortimer returned to the boardroom to offer his apologies for our aborted mission.

'I did not inform him that you were police officers.' He spoke very quietly. 'I simply informed him that two gentlemen had asked to speak to him. The general impression from his work-mates is that he noticed the CID car in the car park and he left immediately, totally without sanction from senior management and without giving a reason to his workmates.'

'Thanks, Mr Mortimer. You did your best. Our duty now is to find him, wherever he is.'

'If he returns, I shall order him to contact you in person,' promised Mortimer.

'You'd be better ringing the police station discreetly,' suggested Rocky. 'We would then come here to speak to him.'

'But I do owe a duty of care and confidentiality to all our staff and have no wish to be a police informer. What Mr Jones does will be his decision, not mine.'

'That is your right, Mr Mortimer, and I thank you for your assistance to date. Come along, DC Rhea, we have a job to do.' And we left.

Without delay, we drove to his mother's address on the edge of town. In her late sixties, white haired but with a very smooth and fresh complexion, she admitted she had no idea where her son might be.

With a hint of Welsh in her accent, Mrs Jones told us, 'So far as I know, he went to work this morning as usual and I don't expect him home until about quarter to five this evening. He finishes work at 4.30. He's not in trouble again, is he?'

'Not to our knowledge, Mrs Jones. We received a call from Leeds City Police to interview Arvin because he has witnessed a serious crime in Roundhay Park. They want him to tell us what he saw, that's all. To our knowledge, he is not in trouble – he's a witness, not a suspect.'

'Really? How nasty to see something like that! He's a kind man, really, loves animals and hates seeing anything being hurt. He would never kill another human being, I'm sure of that.'

'We're not here to accuse him of anything, Mrs Jones, we simply want to know what he saw. Do you mind if we have a look around the house? His bedroom for starters?'

'Well, no, I suppose not but I haven't got round to making the beds yet.'

'That doesn't worry us. Can you lead the way?'

We knew Pat The Butter was large enough to make his concealment almost impossible but we searched his bedroom none the less, including the wardrobes and under the bed; we did likewise in the other two bedrooms, bathroom and toilet, then the loft, all downstairs rooms and the garden shed. There was no sign of him.

'He's not here, Mrs Jones, so when he comes home, can you ask him to contact us? We're at Strensford CID at the police station. I am Detective Constable Salt and this young man is trainee Detective Constable Rhea.'

He wrote our names and the phone number of the police station on a piece of paper and handed it to her.

'You don't think he did it, do you? Killed somebody?'

'Mrs Jones, it did not happen in our area. We have been asked to interview Arvin to get his version of events.'

'All right, when he comes in, I'll tell him to get in touch.'

We left and made our way back to the police station; Rocky had the difficult task of ringing Leeds City Police to say we could not find Jones, adding that we had left messages for him to contact us when he either returned home or resumed work in the shipyard.

The Leeds detective who took our call said, 'So the bird has flown the nest, eh? He's as guilty as hell, gentlemen, so if you keep an eye open for him in Strensford, we'll alert the rest of the country along with the ports, airports and ferries. One way or another, we'll find him.'

When we were alone, Rocky said, 'There's no fault on our part, Nick, but it would be nice if we could be the ones who track him down, whatever he has or hasn't done.'

CHAPTER 12

It was still mid-morning as we found ourselves faced with extending our search for Arvin Jones. We knew he'd keep away from his mother's house until he'd decided we were tired of searching his home; perhaps he would sneak back under cover of darkness. Or he might never come back – he might have friends a long way from Strensford.

'What I don't understand,' said Rocky as we headed for our car, 'is why Leeds asked us to interview him. If they suspected his guilt, surely they'd have sent their own officers to deal with the inquiry?'

'Maybe at the time they rang, they genuinely considered him to be a witness rather than a suspect?' I put forward a suggestion, perhaps a rather weak one.

'But even doing a runner like this doesn't make him guilty, Nick. Whatever his reason for bolting, we have to find him. So where do we go from here? Any ideas?'

'Checking his known local haunts? Pubs, clubs and so on. Pals' houses?'

'That's all got to be done so let's get started. I've known him a long time so we'll start with the Black Lion, that's his favourite watering hole. We might learn something from staff and customers, then we'll take things from there.'

We parked the car and trudged from place to place, amassing a considerable amount of intelligence about the recent movements of The Butter but nothing that could be associated with our current inquiries.

The landlord, staff and customers of the Black Lion were as helpful as they could be but we failed to find even the tiniest hint of his whereabouts or a likely hiding place although we did search the inn, its bedrooms, loft and outbuildings. We took care not to suggest to his friends or colleagues he was wanted for interview about a murder or indeed a crime of any kind; all we said was that we'd like to have a chat with him. Most of those to whom we spoke promised that when they next saw him, they would advise him to get in touch, but we had little faith in such an unreliable system. We would continue in the hope of tracing that elusive clue that sometimes emerged in such cases.

However, after a couple of unproductive hours, we decided to return to the office – we had been out of contact for most of the morning and needed to find out whether there had been any other developments. The radio in our car could not connect with the CID office; it transmitted to the charge office in the town's police inquiry office, whose staff would probably be unaware of CID minutiae.

In addition to our inquiries, however, we knew that uniform patrols in town were looking for The Butter. If he was anywhere in the vicinity we were confident we would find him.

'I thought you two had got lost!' commented DS Latimer when we walked into the office.

'Not us, Sarge, it's The Butter who's lost.' Rocky provided a brief summary of our activities.

'You've checked his usual haunts? As if I need ask!'

'We have,' Rocky affirmed. 'We've checked and searched everywhere. Not a whisper. No one's seen or heard of him since he left work.'

'Well,' commented Latimer, 'I have to say it's not really our problem. That rests with Leeds but we'll have to make a show of looking for him on our patch, particularly as he's done a runner here. We shouldn't have let that happen so you'd better have further words with Leeds City CID, put your hands up and ask what else they want from us.'

'I'll do it now,' said Rocky, and picked up an extension to get a line for Leeds City CID.

As he did so, one of the other phones in the office rang, and I answered it.

'Nick, it's Jim in the front office. We've just had a report of a stolen car. From the staff car park at the shipyard. In view of your current interest in the yard, Sergeant Blaketon felt you should know. It's a green Ford Prefect 1956 model, two doors.' He provided the registration number. 'It belongs to one of the secretaries; she went to get something from it and found the car missing, just a few minutes ago. We've alerted all stations in the county, including motor patrols.'

'I'll pass the word around up here, and we'll inform Leeds City.'

'This is now a full-blown murder hunt,' admitted DS Latimer. 'So let's make sure we get things moving in the right direction.'

He took the phone from Rocky and when he was connected to Leeds City Police Headquarters, asked for CID office because he wanted a discussion with a senior officer about the tactics now to be deployed. The main issue was whether The Butter should be described as a suspected murderer who was wanted for interview or whether they should make the appeal look less dramatic by having him described as a valuable witness. Knowledge of their efforts would not be confined to the police – without a doubt, word of their activities would reach the media and so the public would be alerted.

The reaction of DCI Rounton of Leeds City Police was, 'We've now got good reason to believe he *did* commit the murder in Roundhay Park and in my view his evasion confirms it. We've got to find him before he does something else.'

'We'll go along with that,' said DI Baldwin, who had been listening to the conversations. And so the name of Arvin Jones, a shipyard worker in Strensford, was circulated via the police national network as a man on the run who was wanted for questioning about his links to the murder in Roundhay Park, Leeds. Instead of being earlier described as a witness, he was now labelled a suspect who had since fled from his home area after apparently stealing a Ford Anglia two-door saloon from his place of work. Its description and registration number were also circulated.

The printed circulars that followed would include a mugshot (the most recent photograph in police files) but would not explain the precise nature of the cause of death of the murder victim.

We did not want the courts to believe the suspect, or indeed any of those sad people who falsely admit to crimes, had read the details in newspapers. In any subsequent interviews, his interrogators must allow him an opportunity to offer his explanation of the events that had led to his arrest.

For the police officers of Strensford, whether in uniform or members of the CID, their task involved a further close examination of all The Butter's known haunts. We did not lose sight of the possibility that he might have returned to Strensford. CID members were recalled for a special briefing by Detective Inspector Baldwin. Their tasks would include interrogation of The Butter's friends, neighbours and contacts, the tracking of his recent movements and whereabouts around the time of the murder. It would be necessary to determine whether or not the victim had any previous links with The Butter. His personal background would also be examined in great detail and would be part of CID's inquiries. For Strensford Police, it was necessary to establish whether any outstanding crimes, particularly those in or around the town, could be attributed to The Butter. Inevitably, some unsolved crimes, particularly those involving violence, would be reopened and reviewed to see whether he might now enter the frame as a suspect.

The railway station staff, the bus station personnel and taxi operators would be interviewed to see whether The Butter had left town while any media publicity would ask whether anyone leaving town had picked up a hitchhiker at the material time. Lorry drivers in particular would be asked to co-operate.

As the CID officers were allocated their particular actions, I realized I was not included. DI Baldwin asked me to pop into his office as the others gathered information from the files.

'Sorry I couldn't include you in this, Nick, but all those Ds have a personal knowledge of The Butter which they must draw upon now, and in some cases their informants would not reveal what they know if there is a new kid in attendance. But I do have work for you, here in the office.'

I expressed my understanding in these rather exceptional circumstances and he then pointed to a filing cabinet. It was a four-drawer creation skilfully fashioned from oak and its drawers worked on an amazingly smooth sliding system. And it was packed with old files.

'People refer to this as the dead section, Nick, but I regard it as the living section. These are unsolved serious crimes in Strensford Division – one murder, three attempted murders, two rapes, two attempted rapes, two cases of sacrilege, quite a lot of burglaries and housebreakings along with several serious assaults. In all cases, no one has been brought to justice and in some, no suspect has been identified. All have been committed within the last ten years and whenever we have a period of calm, we take out one of these files and review it, aided by the light of modern knowledge, current techniques and scientific-bloody-aids. For you this afternoon, this is a period of calm, so can you select a file or two and cast your eyes over them? You might produce a name for re-interview, you might spot something we've missed ... can you do that for us? It would be most helpful.'

'Yes, of course, sir, so is there some particular reason for doing this?'

'Yes, it follows today's events. I believe Arvin The Bastard Butter has committed other local crimes for which he has never been caught or even suspected.'

'Recently?'

'Over the years, ever since he was a juvenile. He has been interviewed for several as you'll see from those records but we have never pinned one on him. I need to know what those crimes were, where they were committed and who the victims were – and whether we should take another look at him and his alibis with the Leeds job in mind. If we can name him as a suspect in some of our own cases, he might ask for them to be taken into consideration if he's charged with any recent crime. If he did co-operate, it would seriously aid our crime statistics and detection rate!'

'Cold case reviews?' I asked.

'That's a good name for the files, young Rhea.'

'Isn't there a limitation on the time someone can be prosecuted for a crime after it's committed?'

'In some cases, yes, but not with murder or many other serious crimes. They can be prosecuted without any limitation. It means it would be a great help if you could identify his hand in some of those earlier crimes – you might think it wise to get more information about the current Leeds murder to see if you could spot any matches or similarities. You'd need to speak to

DI Marrick if you find gaps in the material already available, so mention my name if you need to contact him.'

'Of course, sir, I'd love to tackle this.'

'That's what I like to hear. I'll leave the choice of files to you and your judgement. I do not wish to suggest any particular case – and by the way, The Butter is not the suspect for them all! But his MO or his trademark might crop up in one or two.'

'I'll get cracking straightaway,' I assured him.

'Great. Now I must leave and join the others in the hunt – he could still be somewhere in town. I get the feeling that things are hotting up!'

Then he was gone. Suddenly I was alone and the spacious office with its deserted desks and large central table looked surprisingly bleak and abandoned. I felt rather abandoned as I did my best to understand why they had not involved me in the practical aspects of the manhunt – was there any connection with the fact that I had identified a stolen coat two years after commission of the crime? Did they think I possessed a more-than-average acumen when it came to detecting old crimes? Was that why I was hunting through old files? I had no idea, but I had to obey orders.

I picked up the telephone and rang Leeds City Police Headquarters, asking to be put through to Detective Inspector Marrick in CID, giving my name and that of Strensford when requested by the operator.

'Marrick,' responded a voice.

I gave my name, rank and station to him and said, 'I've been asked to contact you, sir, by DI Baldwin. It concerns the recent murder in Roundhay Park.'

'And how is DI Curser Baldwin?'

'Fine, sir, and still cursing.'

'We were together on our Detective Training Course at Wakefield,' he told me. 'He cursed a lot during that course but we became pals. So how can I help?'

'He has asked me to search our undetected files to see whether The Butter might have been responsible for some of the undetected crimes. I know we have the circular about the murder, sir, but I wondered if there was anything else that might help me as I search and review the old files.'

'Such as what?'

'It's hard to say but I know in the case of murder the precise method of killing is not released to the media so as to avoid copy-cat crimes by others, and to avoid false confessions.'

'There are certain police officers who would sell their mothers to make a little extra beer money or cash for betting by selling secrets to the press. So we do have secrets, DC Rhea, and we have not revealed the method of killing the Roundhay Park victim for the reasons you give. I can tell you, though, that our search of the murder scene located a lump of chewed chewing gum. His CRO file refers to his habit of chewing gum and spitting it out while committing his crimes. The trouble was that we couldn't get a match between the teeth marks in the gum and those in his mouth, and he denied any involvement with the murder. However, he did admit to being at the scene – hence the gum. The deceased was local and Jones claims he saw two men running away, but he remained to call the police, asking a passer-by to ring 999. I must admit, DC Rhea, that he told a very convincing story, and if you talk to him you might believe everything he says. The trick, it seems, is to believe nothing he tells us.'

'I didn't know all this.'

'Well, young man, there is no reason why you should know all this, but you know now. Best of luck with your research and I'd be interested in what you turn up from The Butter's past. A fresh young brain analyzing the evidence is a good move and we all might benefit from your efforts.'

'Thank you, I hope so, sir.' He had already replaced the phone.

I went to the filing cabinet and eased out the files relating to The Butter alias Arvin Jones. There were several.

CHAPTER 13

My first self-imposed task was to study further details of the Leeds murder to see if there were any other references to chewing gum. I could begin that by reading the West Riding Crime Informations. This would provide the necessary brief outline of the crime. If I felt I should know more, I could ring Leeds City CID.

WRCIs were daily news-sheets featuring crimes and details of wanted, suspected or missing persons. Recent convictions at assizes and quarter sessions on charges of major crimes were also reported, along with photographs of the offenders. Collated by the staff at the West Riding Police Headquarters at Wakefield, the WRCIs were printed overnight and circulated by police cars early next morning. They were initially distributed to the headquarters of various Yorkshire police forces, York City, Leeds City, Hull City and Sheffield City, as well as the three county forces – East Riding, North Riding and West Riding. They were also despatched to neighbouring counties such as Lincolnshire, Derbyshire, Lancashire, Co. Durham, Cumberland and Westmorland.

When these Crime Informations arrived at a police headquarters they were immediately distributed by night patrols to the divisional headquarters within those force areas for further dissemination to the constituent police stations by not later than 8 a.m. Copies were also sent to New Scotland Yard, as well as the headquarters of the City of London Police, the British Transport Police, the security services, the Ministry of Defence Police and other small specialist police services.

In that well-practised way, their contents were quickly made available nationwide each morning to all oncoming shifts of uniformed police officers and detectives, including those serving in rural areas.

It was a slick, vital and effective system. Police officers, when beginning their shifts, were ordered to be aware of their contents but in fact when we reported for duty, the sergeant would summarize items of local interest, and pass photographs around for us to look at. As the Roundhay Park murder had been committed a few days earlier, the previous Saturday, in fact, I quickly located details published in what we had abbreviated to 'The West Ridings'. The entry featured the traditional police practice of using capital letters for surnames to avoid confusion, especially among some odd or foreign surnames:

MURDER. ROUNDHAY PARK, LEEDS. Deceased: John William EDWARDS, b. 1919 at Pudsey, West Riding of Yorkshire. Sheet Metal Worker. Home Address: 32 Waterford Street, North Wessenden.

The fully clothed body of EDWARDS was discovered in woodland at Roundhay Park, Leeds at 5.30pm, Friday, 16th August 1957. He had been strangled manually at that location. It is not known whether anything had been stolen from the body. Two youths aged 17-20 were observed fleeing the scene and have not been traced. They are wanted for interview.

No.1 aged 17-19. Average height (5'9"), average weight, long dark hair, pale complexion, wearing a short-sleeved shirt, dull green colour with dark brown trousers.

No.2 aged 17-20. Thick set, heavy build, 5'8" tall, long fair hair, pale complexion, wearing short-sleeved shirt light blue colour and blue jeans. Both were seen running from the scene at around 5.30pm.

EDWARDS was married to Elaine and had two children, a boy aged 17 and a girl 15. He had no convictions. Witnesses are sought.

The first thing I noticed was that there was no reference to Arvin Jones alias The Butter and although I searched the following bulletins to see whether he had been later mentioned as a potential witness, I found nothing. When I telephoned Leeds City CID, I thought they had not been particularly helpful – maybe there was an element of distrust in their response – but the fact they had wanted my force to trace, interview and eliminate Jones suggested that evidence of his possible involvement may have developed some time after the murder victim had been discovered. I wondered if the post mortem had provided additional evidence.

As I pondered these events, it became clear to me that, as I served in a different force area and had not been privileged to visit the scene of the murder nor attend the post mortem on the body of the deceased, I was rendered fairly useless in attempting to solve the crime by interviewing Jones. But I had to remind myself, my function was not to solve the murder – it was to find The Butter. The task of identifying and tracing the killer was the responsibility of the Leeds City team. My force were heavily involved in tracing a current suspect simply because he lived in Strensford and had allegedly reported finding the body.

Although I did not have wide police experience, it was commonly believed by police officers that the person who reported finding the body of a murder victim could be the killer, hoping that his 'honesty' would absolve him from suspicion. The truth was that it worked the other way – the person who reported finding a murder victim became an instant suspect who had to be eliminated from suspicion.

I decided to delve into old local files in which he had featured; I was aware that he may have found shelter with friends or family in Strensford and still be hiding in town.

I found three local cases in which The Butter had featured. In one, he had proved himself a hero because a man had snatched a woman's handbag outside Woolworths and had run off with it, only to be stopped by the quick-thinking and vigilant Arvin, who had promptly stuck out his leg to trip the thief. Then he had sat on him until the police arrived. A uniformed constable happened to be patrolling Pier Road and was alerted by the shouting and commotion. He was at the scene within seconds.

The woman's handbag was returned and in court the thief was fined £25 and put on probation for two years. The Butter received high praise in the *Strensford Gazette* with a commendation from the Chairman of the Bench in the magistrates' court.

The other two files contained information that was not so complimentary about Arvin. As a teenager, he had assaulted and robbed a 20-year-old man who was walking home from a Strensford pub after closing time. He had felled his victim with a rabbit-punch to the back of the neck and when he was lying on the ground, rifled through his pockets to steal £12.

Fortunately, both the assaulted man and a witness had recognized The Butter and even though he claimed he had witnessed the assault and driven off the attacker, his story was not believed. The Butter was fined £50 and placed on probation for three years. When the injured man was treated in hospital, however, a lump of chewed chewing gum was found stuck to his hair and it was widely believed that The Butter spat it out during his attack.

A confidential police note in that file said that The Butter was known to be addicted to chewing gum; he chewed it constantly and spat it out whenever he was stressed, angry or confronted by the police. This evidence was exactly the catalyst I needed.

Then I came across another file which told a similar story. Arvin had been noticed standing in an alleyway close to the Working Men's Club in Strensford, chewing gum. The witness thought he was waiting for someone to emerge from the main door. That turned out to be true. When the man did emerge just before midnight, Arvin launched a savage attack, punching him about the head, face and chest and kneeing him in the groin. The man fell to the ground as The Butter ran away, disappearing into the shadows. The injured man required hospital treatment but said he did not want to press charges because Arvin had been seeking revenge for some unspecified act he had committed against The Butter. This incident did not involve a theft.

The file remained open because there had been no prosecution but it served as a reference point because the police visited the scene the following morning in daylight and found two lumps of discarded chewing gum. The incident, as it was described, was recorded in police files because it would serve as a record of Arvin's capabilities and his distinctive way of gaining violent retribution for some unspecified wrong.

If Arvin had genuinely found the Leeds victim, would the stress have caused him to either chew gum or spit it out at the scene? If so, it did not prove he was the killer – if it could be matched to him, it was only evidence he'd been at the scene.

Although I had no claims to be a good detective, and most certainly not an experienced one, I could believe that Arvin may have left some evidence while attacking the man in Roundhay Park. But that was not the reason Strensford detectives were involved in this inquiry; it was because Arvin had given his true home address – another ploy to make him appear innocent?

None of the information possessed by Strensford CID about the Leeds murder referred to his habit or gum at the scene of the crime. I knew that, thanks to that phone call to Detective Inspector Marrick. As I sat and pondered this evidence, I could understand Arvin's reaction when local police wanted to interview him about the murder. In his mind, he would believe they were aware of his guilt and so he had, as they say in police jargon, done a runner to avoid a lengthy interrogation and possible custody. Now I also believed in his guilt – his flight and habit had convinced me that further inquiries were necessary. So where was he? We had not received reports of any sightings as he may have hitched a lift out of town or used the stolen car or perhaps some other available transport.

The car he had stolen from the parking area at the shipyard could be miles away by now. I needed to know if there had been any sightings since it had been stolen, hopefully with a description of the driver. I rang the inquiry office downstairs. A uniformed friend answered.

'It's Nick upstairs, John,' I began.

'Still sleuthing, are you?'

'Doing my best, and I'm thoroughly enjoying it. Now, that car stolen this morning from the shipyard. Have there been any sightings or other news of it?'

'Two sightings,' responded John. 'One from a lorry driver complaining that it was being driven dangerously along the coast road near Sandyford. He was so concerned about it that he recorded the registration number and rang us from a kiosk. We had no spare cars to give chase, but we did notify Traffic. So far, no results from that. Then a few minutes ago a hiker rang from a phone box on the cliffs near Sandyford, saying there was a car on the cliff top, perilously parked overlooking a rocky bay. It matches the description of the stolen car. We've a team on their way right now, and the coastguard is going to have a look.'

'Any report of a man with the car?'

'Nothing. It's standing all alone and empty.'

'Is there any way I can get there?'

'I shouldn't bother if I were you. There's a whole army heading out there: CID, coastguards, a vehicle recovery truck, a Traffic car with a crew of two, and there's also an ambulance standing by. And somebody from the Salvation Army who wants to stop him jumping off the cliff but we've no confirmation that that's the driver's intention. The car seems to have been abandoned but they think the driver is somewhere in the vicinity. He's not at the bottom of the cliff, that's for sure. Not yet, anyway, so stay where you are, Nick – you'd only get in the way and if word of this reaches the great British public, we'll have to cope with a posse of oglers, gawpers and bystanders, not to mention the press.'

'Then I'd better find my new bosses and tell them what's happened.'

The difficulty would be finding my new colleagues for they would have spread themselves around the town, questioning people in places they might expect to find The Butter. They had no portable radio sets and unlike the uniform branch did not make contact points at telephone kiosks. The alternative was to remain in the CID office until one of them returned but as I had no indication of when that might be, I could remain there all day, useless and ineffective. I had to do something.

After a moment's reflection, I decided that one way of contacting detectives currently searching the town for Arvin was to alert them via the uniformed officers currently on patrol. I hurried downstairs to the inquiry office where PC John Fletcher was on duty. I explained the situation and suggested he contact all the constables currently on duty to inform them of this development and pass the news to any CID officers encountered by the uniform patrols. Also, they should maintain observations for Arvin Jones who, in reality, might have staged his own disappearance but who might have returned to his home town to go into hiding. I suggested to John that he also informed the town duty inspector with a view to arranging a search of places where Arvin was likely to take cover while the incident at Sandyford was being dealt with.

'So what are your plans?' he asked me.

'I'm going to visit Uncle Jimmy's Sweet Shop, I have some inquiries to make there.'

'Your excuse for buying some Black Bullets, is it?'

'No,' I responded with as firm a reply as I could muster. 'I'm going to ask about chewing gum. I know Uncle Jimmy keeps some in stock. And I will be looking out for detectives and also for Arvin The Butter. Then I'll come straight back here.'

'If you say so.'

I was confident John would do all in his power to trace and inform the necessary officers. It was a walk of some ten or fifteen minutes to Uncle Jimmy's Sweet Shop and when I arrived, there was no sign of any schoolchildren waiting to be served. Jimmy was behind the counter.

'Good morning, Jimmy.' I introduced myself. 'I'm interested in chewing gum this morning.'

'Oh, we have the town's best selection.' He minced from his place behind the counter to cross the shop to the range of packets on display.

'I don't want to buy any, Jimmy.'

'Oh.' He halted in the middle of the shop.

'I'm here on inquiries. Is Arvin Jones, The Butter, one of your customers?'

'Oh yes, a very good customer, Mr Rhea. A devoted regular, you might say.'

'Has he been in today?'

'It's funny you should mention that, Mr Rhea, but yes, he came in not long ago, twenty minutes or thereabouts. He was in a big rush and was wearing a Kiss Me Quick hat, then he grabbed a fistful of packets of chewing gum and dashed out, saying he would pay me later. He did look distressed, I might add.'

'Did he have a car outside?'

'Not that I was aware of. Is he in trouble, Mr Rhea? He did seem very agitated. But now you mention the car, he didn't have one, he got off a bus, the service that comes from Sandyford and along the coast to Scarborough.'

'Thanks, Jimmy.' I bought a packet of chewing gum and left.

At that point, I guessed where Arvin might be hiding but I felt that locating and then arresting him would require team-work with perhaps the matching weighty presence of Peter Rocky Salt. I decided to hurry back to the CID office; I had to devise a way of passing my theory to the CID team currently operating in the town, and the only way I could think of was to contact one of the CID personnel via the point-making routine of the uniformed officers. I'd be unlikely to encounter any of them if I carried out my own search of the town. Ten minutes later I was in the inquiry office again talking to PC John Fletcher and happily Sergeant Blaketon was present.

I explained my theory after which Blaketon asked, 'So where do you think he is, Nick? The whole area's been searched twice.'

'He'll be in the place where everyone seeks refuge, Sergeant. His mother's house.'

'It's already been searched, Nick. Several times. Nothing there.'

'Including the loft?'

'Including the loft, all the bedrooms, the greenhouse and garden shed. All searched, all with a nil result.'

'When was that?'

'About an hour ago.'

'Well, about half an hour ago, he dashed into Uncle Jimmy's Sweet Shop to get some chewing gum,' I told him. 'He might have gone home to Mum after the searches.'

'Leave it with me, Nick. I'll arrange another search.'

I went upstairs to continue my research in the old files and half an hour or so later DI Baldwin returned to the office.

'We got him, Nick. He wasn't at his mother's but he was at her sister's house next door, in the garden sodding shed.'

'That's a relief!'

'It is. He's in our cells awaiting an escort from Leeds who'll return him to Leeds City CID for further interrogation. It seems they've found some new evidence that will pin the crime on him. Thanks for your input.'

'A pleasure, sir,' I said. 'Fancy a piece of chewing gum?'

CHAPTER 14

ONE FAIRLY COMMON occurrence within the world of local crime reported to the police involves a mistaken belief that a crime has been committed when in fact it has not.

One of my early encounters of this kind occurred in Strensford when I was a uniformed constable, not many months before my attachment to CID. An agitated gentleman of rather advanced years arrived at the inquiry office while I was on early turn in uniform. He knocked on the window of the hatch and shouted, 'Anybody there?'

I was typing a report just around the corner, out of his sight, so called back, 'I'll be with you in a second, sir.'

'This is urgent!' he shouted.

I broke off mid-sentence to attend to him. 'How can I help?'

'That spade thief has been back!' he snapped at me. 'I thought you chaps were going to keep an eye on my garden shed! This isn't the first time, you know. He's been before, stealing my spade so I can't get on with my gardening.'

'I'm fairly new here,' I explained. 'I don't know about those earlier cases.'

'Well, you should have been told! It's a serious matter that's been going on for months. I expect you and your colleagues to guard my shed, and stop the thief or else catch him in the act.'

'There are heavy demands on our manpower, sir. We have many commitments ...' I began.

He ignored my attempt to speak, proclaiming, 'It must be stopped, Constable, I can't afford to keep losing spades! I am a rates payer and I deserve better treatment than this. I know my rights.'

'I'm sure we're doing our best but I'll have a word with the shift sergeant when he returns, and then when PC Johnson takes over from me here in the office, I'll come and examine your shed. I need to visit the scene of the crime and if there has been a break-in, CID will deal with it.'

'Can't you come straightaway?'

'Sorry, no. I'm on office duty for the next half hour. I can't leave the phone, the radio or my inquiry office duties until the duty constable returns after his breakfast break. Something urgent might happen. I'm sure you will understand that I can't leave the office unattended and I'm afraid the theft of your spade does not qualify as an emergency.'

'But something urgent has happened, Constable. Somebody's stolen my best spade.'

'I'll come as soon as I'm replaced here or I can send another officer to deal with your case but it will take time to contact one as they're all out on patrol in town. I need to wait for one of them to make his point so I can contact him. So what's your name and where do you live?'

He said he was Albert Tomlinson and gave an address on the edge of town. He was not at all happy that I refused to leave the police station immediately to find his missing spade but he muttered something and wandered off. It was ten minutes later when Sergeant Blaketon, the shift sergeant, returned from his refreshment break.

'All correct, Rhea?' was his usual opening query.

'No, Sergeant. I've just had the report of a crime, only a few minutes ago.'

'Referred it to CID, did you?'

'No, there was no break-in. A garden spade has been stolen.'

'Not Albert Tomlinson again, was it? Another spade nicked from his shed?'

'Yes, that's the name he gave.'

'That man has reported dozens if not hundreds of spades being nicked from his garden shed, Rhea,' grunted Blaketon. 'I don't know what his insurance company makes of it all but if you take the advice of an experienced policeman, you'll come to realize it has not been stolen.'

'Hasn't it? He was pretty sure it had been.'

'He lends them to friends and neighbours, then forgets who's got them or where they are. When he can't find his spade, he thinks it's been nicked and comes here to report it stolen. In the meantime he buys another, then the borrower usually returns the absent spade when it's served its purpose, so Tomlinson has a garden shed full of spades. He's a one-man crime wave, Rhea, making our crime figures soar into the heavens because he persists in saying they've been stolen. Anyway, when PC Johnson gets back, go and visit the scene. Tell old Tomlinson that every officer at our disposal is now looking for his spade. That should keep him quiet for a while, although it won't be long before he returns to report another spade theft.'

It was about three-quarters of an hour later when I arrived at Albert Tomlinson's bungalow and found him in the garden, mowing the lawn. He stopped his work and came to meet me, walking across a pristine lawn. The rest of the garden was as neat as a show garden, beautiful with flowers and shrubs and not a weed in sight.

'Thank you for coming, Constable. It really is getting to a dreadful state of affairs when a chap can't leave his spades unattended without them being stolen. I don't know what the world's coming to.'

'I'll need to check the shed, Mr Tomlinson, to see if the lock's been forced or whether there was a break-in through the window or wherever.'

'Oh, no, it's nothing like that, Constable. I never lock the door, never have done, there's never been the need around here—'

'Even though someone's sneaking in and stealing spades?'

'Right. You see, Constable, if I padlocked the door and secured the window, then a determined spade stealer would break in and damage the shed while doing so. By leaving the door unlocked, my shed is never damaged. It will be a costly job for me, a pensioner, repairing any damage to that door.'

'I'm not sure I agree with that logic, Mr Tomlinson, but lead me to your shed and show me where the spade was kept. Tell me how it could have been stolen.'

It was a wooden shed, eight feet long or thereabouts, and six feet wide. There was a sliding door and a small window in the eastern end. He eased open the door on a well-oiled runner and showed me the interior. Among all the other garden clutter and tools, there were dozens of garden spades.

'One thing's for sure, Mr Tomlinson, you're not short of a few garden spades! How many are there?'

'At last count, Constable, forty-eight.'

'I'd have thought one was enough for you, so why so many?'

'Well, when I have one stolen or not returned after I've lent it to someone, I have to buy another and it's funny that when I do that, the missing one usually turns up. I keep having them stolen and replacing them, so I have a lot of spades.'

'So why buy another when you've so many? There's enough here to keep the entire park department supplied.'

'It's the insurance. When I claim for a stolen one, they refund me the current value on the understanding I spend it on a replacement. I'm an honest man, Constable, and would never try to cheat the insurance company.'

'You could start a spade-hire business, Mr Tomlinson. Now there's an idea!'

'Oh, I don't know about that, I might never get them back.'

'But there's only one missing, isn't there?'

'At the moment, yes. I have them all numbered, you see.' He showed me the numbers painted in white on the shaft of each spade. 'It's number twenty-five that's been stolen.'

'Are you sure? It could be somewhere among all those others.'

'No, I keep them in numerical order so I can quickly see whether one is missing. And number twenty-five is missing, you can see the gap.'

'And you didn't lend it to anyone or give anyone permission to remove it?'

'Absolutely not, Constable. Someone has taken it without permission, and I call that stealing. Burglary even.'

'Burglary only relates to dwelling houses, Mr Tomlinson, and to commit that crime, the break-in and the stealing must be done at night between nine in the evening and six next morning. So this is not a burglary. Housebreaking occurs during the daytime hours but as I said, this is not a house although the crime can be committed in places within the curtilage of a dwelling house and includes garages, shops, warehouses, schools and similar premises. So we get shop-breaking, garage-breaking, warehouse-breaking and so on. I'm not sure about garden-shed-breaking.'

'I don't understand all that legal stuff, Constable. All I want is to get my spade back.'

'But as I said, you don't need another ...'

'You never know when a spade is needed, Constable.' And then he began to count his collection of spades, reassuring himself that they were all in numerical sequence. I moved out to give him more room to manoeuvre. Then, as if on cue, I heard the garden gate being opened and when I looked towards it I saw a man entering, carrying a garden spade. He hurried across to where I was standing.

'I hope old Albert isn't complaining that I've stolen his spade again, is he? He's done that before, you know, loaned me a spade for a week or two, forgotten all about it and then accused me of stealing it.'

'We know about him at the station.' I accepted the spade. 'My sergeant suggested I come here to see the situation if it happens again.'

'Which it will,' said the newcomer. 'It might be easier if I bought my own but I've such a tiny garden …'

As we were speaking, Albert came to the door, looked at the man and the numbered spade, and said, 'There we are, Constable, caught in the act.'

I took the spade from the visitor and said to him in a loud voice, 'Thank you for bringing the spade back, sir, I'm sure Mr Tomlinson didn't intend leaving it in the back lane.'

'Thanks,' the man said to me as he handed over the spade. 'I'll buy one for myself now.'

'You can borrow this one if you want,' suggested Albert, ignoring my reference to the back lane.

'No thanks, Albert, it's very kind of you but I really think I need one of my own now.'

'No,' insisted Albert. 'I've a shed full of spades and can't use them all at once, so you can keep that one, I don't need it.'

'I'll pay for it.'

'No need, just give a donation to the lifeboat,' suggested Albert.

'You're a witness to all this, Constable,' said the man, who turned to Albert and said, 'Thanks, Albert, you're a gent. I'll drop half a crown into the lifeboat box at the pub.'

'Well,' I said. 'All's well that ends well. Now I must get back to the office.'

A fortnight later, Albert returned to the police station to complain that his neighbour had stolen his spade ... but I was not on duty at that time.

I grew more confident as the days went by and found CID work interesting and worthwhile – and it certainly wasn't without its humorous moments. One afternoon I answered the phone in the CID office. It was Sergeant Blaketon calling from the inquiry office downstairs.

'Ah, DC Rhea.' He sounded very formal. 'I have a lady at the inquiry desk who has witnessed a crime. I think this is for your department. Can someone come and speak to her?'

'I'm alone at the moment, Sergeant. The others are all out.'

'Then *you* must deal with this witness,' and he replaced the phone.

I hurried downstairs and into the inquiry office where Sergeant Blaketon and PC John Cummins were on duty. A woman, smartly dressed in a dark suit, whom I guessed was in her late fifties or early sixties, was sitting on a chair inside the office, clearly in a state of some distress. She was clutching a mug of tea.

'Ah, DC Rhea.' Blaketon used my formal name. 'This is Mrs Palmer from Edinburgh, she is visiting Strensford. I think it would be advisable if you talked to her in the muster room; it is not in use at the moment.'

'Follow me,' I invited her. 'I am Detective Constable Rhea.'

'Thank you.' She was weeping quietly to herself and whispered hoarsely. Clearly she was in distress and I wondered why a woman police officer had not been called to attend to her.

The muster room was where the uniformed officers assembled for their briefings before going on duty. In the centre was a large table with ten chairs around it and ancient pictures on the walls, probably inherited from the private house that had previously occupied this old building. I settled her on a chair at the end of the table but she declined my offer of a refill for her mug of tea. Then I opened one of the drawers and withdrew a few statement forms that were kept in there. I guessed I would need to take a written statement from her, whatever the problem.

'So, Mrs Palmer, will you tell me what's happened? I won't write anything down just yet but I do need to know the full story.'

Now she was rather more composed but still sniffing tears away as she whispered, 'It was so upsetting … so awful …' And she blew her nose. 'Maybe you think I'm being silly …'

'If it's something that has upset you this much, it can't be silly,' I said.

She took a few deep breaths. 'It's the first anniversary of my mother's death. She lived here and is buried in St Hilda's churchyard. I came down from Scotland to put some flowers on her grave and to remember her at a memorial service in church …'

I nodded, not interrupting but giving a sign for her to continue when she was ready. 'The service is not until tomorrow but this morning I went to the churchyard to put some flowers on her grave …'

She paused again and I waited.

'When I entered the churchyard via the lychgate, I saw a woman … she was stealing flowers from the graves, Mr Rhea, I saw her. Going round the graves and carrying bunches away. I shouted something but she hurried away and left via a small gate behind the church. I didn't know what to do … I was so upset, it's such an awful thing to happen … I tried to compose myself, tended my mum's grave. There was no one in the church I could tell about the thief, so I thought I should come here to report it …' She burst into tears again. 'But can you believe anyone could be so awful as to steal flowers from graves?'

'It's a shocking thing to do,' I agreed with her. 'I've never come across this sort of thing in Strensford but I shall look into it immediately.'

'Thank you. I wondered if I was being silly reporting it but felt I had to …'

'It's not at all silly, you did absolutely the right thing. Now, I need a contact address whilst you're here, and your home address to let you know what happens if you've returned to Scotland before we get this sorted out.'

'I understand.' Her tears had dried a little.

'Right now, though, I need a written statement for you to sign. I need that for our crime file. And I need a description of the woman. I will ask the vicar and others who use that church, or indeed other churches in Strensford, to see whether or not this kind of thing has been reported before. It is a crime of larceny, the legal word for theft, Mrs Palmer, and it will be dealt with as such.'

After saying she was sure of the time the crime was committed – 9.30 a.m. – Mrs Palmer could not provide a very detailed description of the woman. She excused herself by saying she had been too disgusted and shocked to note anything distinctive about the thief. However, she could say was that she was a woman of average height and build, probably in her fifties, with light brown but greying hair. Her hair was quite short, certainly not shoulder-length, and she was not wearing a hat. She was wearing a grey and red skirt with a white top. She thought the woman was wearing sandals rather than high heels because she moved so quickly. As it was a fine, bright, sunny morning, she did not have an overcoat or umbrella. She did not see her again after she had hurried away through the small gate behind the church.

I wrote her account of the event in longhand on a statement form and she signed it as a true account. I told her I would go immediately to the vicarage which adjoined St Hilda's Anglican Church to ask if the vicar was aware of such thefts and would then ask at other churches in town. When I had more information, I would contact Mrs Palmer at her lodgings. She seemed to be more composed having told someone of her experiences and left with a brief smile and a thank you.

I used the police station bike to ride the mile or so to St Hilda's Church and its nearby vicarage. Although the church was open, there was no one inside and so I went to the vicarage and rang the bell. A woman answered – and she matched the description of the flower-stealing suspect. My heart missed a beat but I needed to speak to the vicar. Was she his wife? Or secretary? A church cleaner?

'I am Detective Constable Rhea from Strensford Police Station.' I showed my warrant card. 'Could I speak to the vicar, please? It's urgent and important.'

'Come into the drawing room, I'll see if Mr Lang is available. I am his wife, by the way.'

After settling me down, she went into the depths of the massive old house and returned with the vicar, who used a chair opposite.

'I'll arrange coffee. You would like a coffee, Mr Rhea?'

'Thank you, yes.'

'So, Mr Rhea, how can I help the constabulary?' The Reverend Lang was a tall, rather handsome man with greying hair and an athletic build. He was formally dressed in a dark suit, black shoes and a clerical collar.

I related Mrs Palmer's story without giving a description of the suspect thief, and could then see the growing amusement on the faces of both the vicar and his wife. She had not yet left us to make the coffee but in those few moments I understood what Mrs Palmer had witnessed. I felt a bit of an idiot for not realizing earlier.

'It's just dawned on me what was happening …' I felt a bit flustered.

'Not to worry, Mr Rhea, you are not the only person to have questioned us about this but my wife – Beatrice – goes around the graveyard at least once a week or more, removing all the dead or dying flowers from the graves.'

'Of course, someone has to do it!'

'If you want to see them, they are on our compost heap in the far corner of the graveyard, through that little gate …'

'I shall take your word for that!' I smiled with some relief. 'I know that few people bother to remove their own spent flowers.'

And so the supposed theft was not a crime. When I rang Mrs Palmer at her boarding house she was both amused and relieved at the outcome, and said she would visit the church to make a donation for the flowers at her mother's memorial service.

CHAPTER 15

A VERY PREVALENT crime during the late 1950s and early 1960s involved the unlawful taking of motor vehicles. This was not classified as larceny, the word then used for theft, because there was no intention to *permanently* deprive the owner of the vehicle. Permanent deprivation was an essential ingredient in theft/larceny.

'Taking without consent' was the unauthorized borrowing of a motor vehicle, known in police jargon as TWOC. The police often talked of people twocking motor vehicles or cars being twocked.

One could TWOC any kind of motor vehicle but not machines without engines, such as bicycles or prams. I don't think TWOC applied to steam rollers, traction engines, children's scooters, boats or steam engines on the railways.

It was a regular feature in most towns that bicycles were borrowed without consent, often to transport someone home from the pub, but this was not catered for in criminal law. Certainly it was, and still is, a crime to *steal* a bicycle, but unauthorized borrowing is not classified as theft even if it infringes civil law. However, once people hit on the idea, and indeed the convenience, of unauthorized borrowing of cars, vans, lorries etc., the law had to be amended to accommodate this dishonesty.

Such borrowers were able to take the vehicles even though there was no key in the ignition. I recall from the early 1950s that the ignition key of one particular model of saloon car was quite capable of opening the doors and starting the engine of other makes. On one occasion I found an abandoned stolen Humber Snipe in a car park while I was on night duty and after it had been examined by CID for fingerprints and other evidence, I drove it to the police station yard for safe-keeping by starting it with the ignition key from my own 1938 Austin 10. And, of course, the skill of 'hotwiring' could start a car without an ignition key while it was a well-known trick in those days that a locked car could be entered with the skilful use of a wire coathanger.

I once used this trick when I was performing uniform duties at York Races. A television personality had locked herself out of her car and came to me for help. Fortunately, she was carrying some spare clothing on a wire coathanger, which I twisted into a hook, inserted through a gap between her car door and the bodywork and unlocked the door by lifting the internal door handle. It was not uncommon for people to lock themselves out of cars at that time, nor indeed for some householders to lock themselves out of their homes.

In such cases, police officers were usually contacted to show people how to break into their own homes. These were salutary lessons in how easy it was to break into houses and cars – in other words, that assistance proved to be a good crime-prevention demonstration. It would not work with twenty-first century locks on houses and cars.

It was quite common for thieves to commit crimes of house-breaking, theft or burglary in, say, the south of England or the Midlands, and then take a car from a town centre car park or street. They would drive the car for a short distance and then, probably before its absence had been noticed, leave it in another car park twenty or thirty miles away. From there, another car would be taken and driven a similar distance before being abandoned and in this way a criminal could travel the length of England at no cost to himself while leaving behind a trail of unlawfully borrowed vehicles.

In those days, when a motor vehicle was either stolen or taken without consent, its registration number and description were immediately circulated to all patrolling police officers whether on foot or motor patrol. Obviously, there had to be some selection – a car stolen or unlawfully taken in, say, Brighton, might never reach the north of England, and so circulation of the details was mainly done on a county or regional basis. Each police force maintained its own daily list of such vehicles and an updated Stolen Vehicle Index was regularly published. The vehicles were considered 'stolen' until the contrary was proved.

From time to time, motor patrol officers would set up road blocks on routes most likely to be used by unlawfully driven vehicles. All approaching drivers would be halted and questioned, and the police officer's first task upon opening the driver's door was to remove the ignition key so he could not drive off. If the vehicle had not been reported missing, perhaps because its owner was still at work, the police officer might sometimes rely on the simple device of asking the driver to state the registration number of the vehicle he was sitting in; if he did not know its number, it had probably been unlawfully taken.

Generally, CID officers did not investigate stolen or unlawfully taken vehicles; their recovery almost always depended upon a uniformed patrol officer spotting the vehicles either being driven or left abandoned somewhere with or without false registration plates. Once found, however, scenes of crime officers would examine the vehicles for fingerprints or other evidence but that was usually their only involvement.

However, CID did maintain files of expensive vehicles – cars, classic cars, agricultural vehicles, etc. – being stolen to order and perhaps driven to the ferries before they had been missed, then to be exported to European and Asian dealers. Nonetheless, the main task of tracing such vehicles often depended upon the uniform branch spotting the vehicles in use on the roads or abandoned somewhere, even in someone's drive or an official car park.

One of the most tempting of instances for a car thief arises when someone leaves an unattended car parked with the key in the ignition and the engine running. People often do this when posting a letter or buying a daily paper. This happened to a young mother in a Teesside town. I did not deal with this crime but news of it was circulated rapidly to police officers throughout the north-east of England and inevitably it reached the news media.

That young woman, whom I shall call Sandra, urgently wanted some medicine from the chemist's and so she drove into town from her house on an estate in the outskirts. Her husband had bought a small car for her to use when he was at work and as she motored through the busy town centre, wondering where she could park for just a few seconds, she noticed a space outside Boots. It was ideal for her little car even if it meant leaving it in a 'No Parking' area for the briefest of moments. She slid into the space but left the ignition key in the lock and the engine running. This was her silent message to any patrolling official that she was dashing into Boots and would be out very soon. She felt a passing policeman would be sympathetic – this was before the days of traffic wardens – as her six-month-old daughter was lying in a carry-cot on the rear seat, fast asleep. I am sure any police officer would have been sympathetic in those circumstances.

But she hadn't bargained for a shoplifter on the run. The

thief had been into Boots and stolen an electric razor. He was fleeing from the store detective just as Sandra was entering. She stepped aside to avoid the two running men.

The thief led the race outside – where a little car with its engine running was conveniently waiting. It was the work of a moment to leap into the car and drive off, with the store detective noting its registration number before it was lost in the town traffic. Meanwhile, Sandra heard her car being driven off and turned round to see it vanishing among the traffic ... with her sleeping baby on board.

She had no idea the man standing near the empty space was a store detective but she screamed, 'Stop him, he's got my baby! My baby's in the car! You must stop him!'

'Your car?'

'With my baby in the back seat ...'

'Come with me, I'll ring the police.'

And he rushed back into the shop.

It took a few moments for him to relate the story to the duty officer at the police station but he was alert enough to sense a great danger to the child – men who dumped stolen cars were not careful where they got rid of them, even driving them into rivers or over cliffs. What had been a routine shoplifting had suddenly became a major drama.

The frantic Sandra shouted and screamed; the store detective remained at her side as, only moments later, a police patrol car roared to a halt beside them. Fortuitously, it had been patrolling in the vicinity and was double-crewed. A policewoman rushed to Sandra's side to comfort her but also to get more details of the baby, its cot and the car as her colleague roared away to join the search.

'We were nearby, all our patrols have been alerted,' she told Sandra. 'Come inside.'

'No!' she screamed. 'I want to be here! I want to be here when he realizes he's got a baby in the car and brings her back ... my baby ...'

But the car never came back.

Half an hour later, with Sandra distraught and sobbing but still standing outside Boots, the news came that her car had been found abandoned in a side street at the other side of town. The ignition key was in the lock but more importantly, her baby was safe, still asleep in her carry-cot on the rear seat. There was no sign of the thief or the stolen razor. Sandra's story was featured in the *Evening Gazette* and on national television and although her baby was unharmed, the news coverage was sufficient to alert many other drivers to the dangers of leaving the key in a parked car's ignition system even for the briefest of moments, especially with the engine running.

The thief was never traced and it is not known whether he ever realized he had carried a baby in that car. But drivers did, and still do, leave their vehicles unattended with the engines running for short times as they dash into a shop or to the toilet. And many get stolen or twocked.

Another example of twocking occurred during my short attachment to the CID as an aide.

The Cottage Hospital at Strensford was not equipped to deal with forensic post mortems and if a case arose where such an examination was required, the corpse was transported to a hospital in Middlesbrough where all the necessary facilities and forensic experts were available. If the local police had to deal with a sudden death where a post mortem was ordered by the coroner, then it would be conducted at Middlesbrough Hospital.

The round journey was more than sixty miles and took about an hour each way, allowing for traffic congestion. During my uniform duty, I had accompanied many deceased persons upon that journey – we had to attend post mortems to witness them as part of the continuity of evidence, and to provide proof of identity of the deceased for the inquest. We travelled with the corpse in an anonymous-looking van that belonged to the hospital, and the vehicle had its own driver.

On one memorable occasion, however, an elderly woman died in Strensford while in the care of the Cottage Hospital, and the prevailing rules for such events demanded a forensic post mortem. I will call her Annie. The anonymous little van from the forensic department of Middlesbrough Hospital was despatched with its usual driver to collect Annie's body from Strensford. It would return later in the day and this was a regular trip for the driver; he was familiar with the route.

At that stage, this was not a police matter and we were not involved. However, as the driver was approaching Middlesbrough, he found himself urgently needing to go to the toilet and hurried to the nearest public conveniences. A man came out as he galloped inside. He had left the keys in the ignition of his van with the engine running. You can now guess what happened.

When the driver emerged, much relieved, only a minute or so later, his van had vanished – along with the contents. At first, he did not believe it – he thought it was one of his colleagues playing a joke – but it did not take him long to realize someone had stolen his van with a dead body on board. There were no logos on the van to indicate its owners or its purpose, and the body was carried in a large coffin-shaped box known as 'the shell', which was strapped to the floor to prevent it sliding about.

The driver, who shall remain anonymous, searched the area around the toilets, but there was no sign of the van or the shell containing Annie. From a nearby telephone kiosk, he dialled 999 to report the theft and waited for the police to arrive; meanwhile he phoned his office at the hospital to break the news to his boss. I have no record of what was said during that interchange but understand from reliable reports that the air turned blue. The hospital sent a car to collect the driver and then awaited the outcome of the police search for the missing van and its peaceful passenger.

Back in the mortuary office, the driver recounted his experiences to his boss, who threatened him with dismissal or worse if the van and its load were not located. My involvement was slight – I had to visit Strensford Cottage Hospital, not in uniform, to speak to the registrar and acquaint him with the full facts of what was happening as the search intensified. I had been given a phone number to call at the Middlesbrough Hospital so that I could keep up to date by periodically ringing from the Cottage Hospital.

All I could say when I arrived was that the vehicle and its contents had not been traced but the search was continuing. At this early stage, Annie's relatives had not been informed of the theft but they were awaiting the outcome of the post mortem – the registrar apologized and said there had been an unforeseen delay and he would keep them informed.

It would be around my fourth or fifth phone call when I received some good news. The missing van and its contents had been found safe and sound in the public car park at the Middlesbrough Hospital, and it was being examined by a scenes of crime team. The post mortem on poor Annie would proceed, if a little later than planned.

The thief was never identified but it was apparent that once he had discovered what lay inside the shell, he had headed for the hospital.

It emerged later that an anonymous phone call had been received at the hospital switchboard from a public kiosk to say a van with a body inside was in the hospital's public car park. The operator had reported the call but had dismissed it as a hoax until news of the theft came through.

The van driver kept his job although he was examined by doctors, who thought he might be suffering from amnesia.

CHAPTER 16

DURING MY ATTACHMENT to CID I was encouraged, during my quieter moments, to familiarize myself with the specialist files, including some very sensitive ones. Although permitted to read them, I was warned never to reveal the contents. I was not allowed to read those marked 'Secret', most of which were concerned with national security, particularly during World War II. I had no wish to know what secrets they contained. If I did not know, I could not reveal the contents, however accidentally that might occur.

Their contents were known only to those carrying the rank of superintendent and higher and as World War II had not long been over at that time – a little more than ten years – some of our British citizens were suspected or even known to have collaborated with the enemy. They were not ignored by the authorities – instead, they were covertly watched; their mail was intercepted and read before delivery, their phones were tapped and other devices were used to ensure the British authorities kept ahead of the enemy. Some of those traitors played a splendid but unwitting role in helping the Allies to win the war.

Much to my surprise, what did emerge from the confidential files was the large number of convicted murderers currently living and working in Strensford. I discovered nine whose ages ranged from early thirties to eighties, and in many cases their names had been changed and a new identity with a back-story had been created. All had been convicted of murder in the English courts, and all had served their sentences either in whole or in part, and then been released on licence under the Prison Act of 1952.

That meant they were never totally free – the conditions of their licences meant that if they committed any further crime, not necessarily murder, they could be recalled to prison.

The presence of one such killer was revealed to the police when he parked his car in a one-way street and it caused a traffic obstruction. His offence was reported by a diligent constable with a view to prosecuting him in Strensford Magistrates' Court. When his previous record was checked, it was discovered he had been convicted of murder some years earlier. He was currently out on licence and working in a furniture store, dealing with members of the public. None was aware of his past.

The superintendent decided not to prosecute for such a petty offence in case it revealed the offender's previous history and so he received only a written caution advising him to be careful where he parked in the future. There was no suggestion that the town's patrolling police officers knew of his past record; it was known only to a handful of senior officers and so his secret was safe. Discreet inquiries later showed he was a really nice man, well respected by all who came into contact with him. He was also good at his job and charming with the customers even though, several years earlier, he had killed his young wife with a carving knife.

None of the other killers out on licence had come to the notice of the police for recent crimes and so we could only assume they were good citizens even if their criminal records indicated otherwise. Whether or not their time in custody had changed their attitudes was a question for the academics but I can say that the police, knowing of their past, did not harass them or reveal their secrets. Release on licence seemed to be a very satisfactory and workable solution to the problem of which penalties suited particular crimes. Few convicted murderers reoffended.

But then something happened that revealed the past of one of our local killers who had been out on licence for many years. He was far from happy about it; he had settled well into a fulfilling life free from crime and had many friends.

The background to this story involved a convicted killer whose home address was Sheffield. While serving his sentence, he had attacked another prisoner with a hammer, which he had smuggled in from the prison workshop. The reason for the attack was not known but it was sufficiently serious to be prosecuted under section 18 of the Offences Against the Person Act of 1861 and he was sentenced to an additional fourteen years in prison. At that time, he had been approaching the date of his release on licence but his additional sentence had halted that. He faced a long term in prison.

However, he escaped from the prison van returning him from court, attacking both the driver and his colleague with such ferocity that they needed hospital treatment. Then he had disappeared. That was ten days earlier and nothing had been seen or heard of him since.

His escape had featured in police circulars and also in the newspapers and on national news, but it seemed he had either gone to ground or managed to flee overseas. The prison authorities were under fire for allowing such a dangerous and known killer to escape during what was a regular and routine operation, and police were being criticized for not tracing him. Then I noticed one of his photos in the *Daily Mail* and suddenly found myself feeling shocked.

I hurried to the CID files of convicted murderers currently living in Strensford either on licence or having completed their sentences, for it was one of those that I recalled when I saw the mugshot of the escapee. Here I must use false names to conceal the identities of the key players in this drama so I shall call my Strensford killer Dick Turpin and will refer to the escapee as William Nevison, nicknamed Swift Nick by Charles II. They were a pair of real highwaymen, vicious robbers who should never have been featured in fiction as romantic and handsome.

It was no trouble finding a photograph of 'Turpin', the murderer now living in Strensford, and as I spread the file before me, DI Baldwin appeared at my shoulder and asked, 'Hot on the trail of something, are we, Nick?'

'I'm not sure, sir, but I just want to match this picture with the one in our file.' I had the *Daily Mail* on the desk before me.

'It's the same bloke!' he said.

'I don't think so: ours is a free man, living in the community on licence and doing a good job of work. We would have known if he had moved away or was serving another sentence.'

'We would indeed so who is this guy?' He pointed to the newspaper.

'He's the one who recently escaped from a prison van after attacking the guard and driver, we've had recent circulars and there's a big hunt for him. He's vanished, gone overseas or gone to ground here. He was doing time for first murder when he attacked an inmate with a hammer, seriously injuring him. Then he attacked his guard in the prison van and escaped after his second trial.'

'Right, I'm with you so far, Nick. What are you trying to tell me?'

'Judging by their photographs, they could be twins.'

'Do we know that?'

'I must admit I've seen nothing in our files to suggest it. Their surnames are different but villains often use false names and identities …'

'So what's the point you're making?'

'If a man wants to go into hiding, what better place than the home of his double? If they are identical twins and play their cards right, how will anyone know that there are two men in the house, not just one? All they must remember is not to be seen together.'

'You're suggesting he's here in Strensford, after all this publicity?'

'He needs to hide, sir, to get himself out of circulation but remain free. We'd never know he was here, would we? How could we know? Any sightings would lead to his twin.'

He paused and I could see he was deciding how to tackle this impending dilemma. 'Then we'd better find out what's really happening. This calls for more than a little subterfuge. Leave it with me, I'll get the matter sorted, and if there's an arrest in the offing, you should make it. It would be your first as a CID man, eh? And a murderer too! You might like to tackle him to chalk up the arrest, although on second thoughts we might need armed police or at the very least the police dogs if we're to bring in either or both of those ruffians.'

I left the office knowing that DI Baldwin would attend to the matter and walked into town to make inquiries about a series of thefts from a clothes shop. It was Boothby's in the main street. Baby-wear was being targeted with small items like woollen bootees, woolly hats, cardigans and so forth being spirited out of the shop on a fairly regular basis. The store had tried to halt the thefts by placing the targeted goods at the rear of the shop on elevated shelves so that they were in constant view of the staff who served at the counters. Self-service in such shops was just becoming fashionable but not every shop had adopted that system. There were grumbles that too many shoplifters were at work.

That morning, our West Riding circulars had highlighted a

team of shoplifters who travelled by train from Leeds and were targeting clothes shops in coastal towns. I had decided to warn our local shops that they might receive a visit in the near future.

Boothby's employed a store detective, a former policewoman called Sue Watkins, and she had had some success but the thefts continued. The snag was that suspected thieves could be challenged only when they had left the store – if inside the shop with the goods in their possession, they could argue they intended to pay. Temptation arose because the long, wide counters carried displays of smaller items and it was known that shoplifters worked in teams, with one distracting the attention of the staff while the other quickly concealed a stolen item about the body, in a bag or even within an item already paid for. That the thieves were skilled operators was never in doubt.

One of my tasks that morning was to warn Sue of the likely arrival of the gang from Leeds but as I approached the wide double doors of Boothby's, they suddenly opened and out dashed a young woman carrying a large shopping bag. Sue was hard on her heels, but the young woman quickly passed the bag to a fellow conspirator who was waiting in the street, and they split to run in opposite directions. Momentarily, Sue did not know which one to chase – but I did.

In fact, I did not need to chase her. She was running towards me as I stood near a lamp-post, apparently waiting for someone, and I halted her by the simple procedure of sticking out my foot to trip her. It worked. She tumbled over my leg but managed to cling onto the shopping bag as she hit the ground.

'I'm awfully sorry,' I apologized as I went to help her to her feet, during which time Sue arrived.

'Nice one, Nick.' She smiled as she seized the arm of the thief and took the bag from her. 'Now this thief is going to visit the manager. Thanks. You're under arrest,' she told the woman, then delivered the official caution beginning with, 'You are not obliged to say anything ...'

'I was just on my way to see you,' I managed to tell her in the commotion. 'To warn you of shoplifters from Leeds.'

I returned to the CID office to learn that DI Baldwin had opted to address a meeting of his staff at 2 p.m. but had not yet informed the others of its content and purpose. As I had some minor inquiries to complete in town I went about my business until lunchtime, after which I returned to the office where everyone was gathering. Copies of the newspaper mugshot of the escapee and our own official photograph of one of our local convicted murderers were waiting at our place settings. At two o'clock we all sat around the big table, all but me wondering about the purpose of the gathering.

Baldwin wasted no time. 'In front of each of you,' he began, 'there are two photographs. You will recognize our local killer who lives here under the new name and identity given to him upon his release on licence; his real name, not for public consumption, is William Bray. You'll be aware that a prisoner called Brian Bray has seriously attacked a warder and escaped from a prison van. He was serving time for murder. You'll probably have worked out now that these two are brothers; not only that, they are twin brothers and you'll see from these photographs that they are like two peas in the proverbial pod.'

He paused as we examined our photographs then continued, 'It is possible that Brian will give the impression of fleeing overseas while in reality he could hide at William's home. This might not be a permanent arrangement – once the fuss has died down, he might finalize his plans by heading overseas, even on his brother's passport.'

'Do we know that for sure, boss?' asked one of the officers. 'Or is this speculation? Have we any intelligence to support that probability?'

'None, but I regard it as highly probable based on the fact they are identical twins. Brian will be seeking a refuge somewhere – his twin brother's house is a possibility, nothing more than that, but we can't ignore it. We have to keep the place under surveillance, which is why we're here now. We have to maintain round-the-sodding-clock observations on William's house. And while we are doing that, we cannot ignore the gravity of their crimes – both are violent men although William has mellowed and led a decent life since his release on licence. In view of recent events that you're familiar with, he might not be very pleased if his notorious brother turns up on the doorstep. In fact, he might already be there.'

He waited for us to absorb the growing import of his words, and continued with, 'Most of the observations will fall on our shoulders, and we have an offer from a special constable whom I know well. His house – Cliff View – is directly opposite William's; he's got a spare bedroom we can use and the house has a rear entrance from a back lane that means we won't be seen coming and going. The intelligence received so far is that Brian is still hiding somewhere and may soon make his move. I've had words with Arthur Askey, who will allow me to use some of the uniform branch in civilian clothes for observation duties. The dog section will be on standby in case we have to raid William's house.'

DI Baldwin went on to say that observations would begin that night at dusk and he nominated Sherlock Watson to take the first shift from 10 p.m. until six the next morning. He must keep a detailed record of the comings and goings at William's house across the road, and cameras with night vision would be issued to record such movements. Sherlock would be relieved by DC Paul Campbell who would watch from 6 a.m. until 2 p.m. with DC Peter Salt taking the back shift from 2 p.m. until

10 p.m. They were ordered to take sufficient refreshments for their duties, and all would be equipped with portable radio sets tuned in to Strensford's police wavelength.

The special constable whose house they were using was a Mr John Hodgson who lived there with his wife; he was a fireman by profession and had been briefed about his part in the operation. The simple message was not to be seen by either of the twins but to report any developments or moves they made. If it was shown that Brian Bray had moved in, then Control would be notified by radio and an operation involving police dogs and armed officers would be mounted with the intention of capturing but not killing him.

Whether his brother had willingly agreed to shelter Brian would be determined and if so he would also be arrested as an accessory.

I was not delegated for any of these duties and readily understood they must be carried out by very experienced officers; I would continue with my normal duties as an aide to CID, learning as I went along.

To cut short a long story, Brian Bray arrived at his brother's house at two o'clock on the first morning of our observations. Sherlock recorded and announced his arrival and the team, now alert and fully complemented with armed officers and police dogs, waited until the lights opposite were extinguished, an indication he had gone to bed in his brother's house. The raid was successfully completed without any shots being fired and both twins were arrested.

Not one for lavishing praise upon his subordinates, DI Baldwin thanked us all and said he would buy us all a pint when the matter was concluded and when the brothers were safely behind bars once again.

'You've still not made your first arrest as a D,' he said to me later. 'But thanks for your input in this operation. Yours was the sort of observational skill that helps to find stolen raincoats. Most useful.'

'Thank you, sir,' was my response.

CHAPTER 17

ONE OF THE noticeable trends during my early weeks with the CID was the high number of thefts from motor vehicles. With many older houses not having garages, private cars and vans were obliged to park on the streets or in designated car parks. That meant they were vulnerable and if their owners left valuables in them, they proved a real temptation to prowling thieves whether the contents were personal property such as cameras and binoculars, or tools and equipment used by tradesmen.

In many older vehicles, there was little protection against determined thieves. They either stole the vehicle itself or something it was carrying, the thefts ranging from cash left in cars for emergencies or parking fees, to attaché cases containing valuable samples displayed by salesmen and saleswomen to potential customers, such as jewellers, watch-makers, chemists and such.

Tourists were frequently targeted, especially if they parked in isolated places on the moors or near a quiet beach. Some would want to stretch their legs and get some fresh air during a long journey, but if they parked in well-known beauty spots and went for a short walk, even only a matter of minutes, their cars were at risk. Thieves prowled such places, knowing that if a tourist parked and left the vehicle, he or she would be away for some time.

The car might be packed with suitcases and even holiday money. There were many instances of tourists' cars being broken into and holiday cash being stolen, just through forgetfulness or carelessness by the owners. I recall a woman's handbag being stolen from a car parked in a lonely beauty spot on the moors, and among its contents was £450 in notes, the family's holiday money. At the time, that was around a police constable's salary for an entire year.

Also at risk were tradesmen's vans. If, say, a plumber, carpenter, painter and decorator, motor mechanic, even a butcher or any similar self-employed tradesman left his van unattended and not within the safety of a garage at night, he ran the risk of it being broken into and valuable tools or stock being stolen.

Some van owners would display a notice informing thieves that no money or valuables were left in the vehicle and that all tools had been removed. In some such cases, the van itself was then stolen.

It was such a dilemma that befell Claude Jeremiah Greengrass on a visit to Strensford to collect some scrap metal from the shipyard. Although he lived some distance away on the moors at Aidensfield, visits to Strensford shipyard were among his regular calls, where he provided a useful service by clearing away unwanted metal in all its maritime forms. No one was sure what he did with such a mass of unwanted stuff but it seems he had a business outlet whose customers would pay for junk. For example, I believe he did a good trade in discarded anchors as garden ornaments while old propellers from ships or even aircraft made useful garden seats, although I never knew how they were created.

On one occasion, I was walking from my digs to the police station when Claude's old truck pulled into the parking area just outside the police station. I noticed its rear area was empty as he jumped out and hailed me.

'Now then, young Detective Constable Rhea, I have a crime for you to detect.'

'Are you admitting something?' I asked, tongue in cheek.

'Now that is not very becoming of a young detective. No, I am not admitting anything, I never do. But I am the victim of a serious crime and I want you and your colleagues to do something about it.'

'Then you'd better come into the station and the duty constable will take particulars.'

'I don't want just any constable to deal with me, I demand the best. If I have had a crime committed against me, then I must have the most experienced officer to sort it out.'

'That rules me out, Claude, I'm only undergoing CID training. Sergeant Blaketon will be on duty, I can refer you to him. Or PC Alf Ventress, he's got loads of experience of dealing with local crimes. Come along, follow me inside, I'll take you to the inquiry office.'

'You don't think I'm going voluntarily into a police station, do you? I have my pride, you know,' and he blinked fast and furiously as he stood before me.

'Claude, if you want to report a crime, you must do it properly and that means making a formal report by supplying the necessary details. There are procedures to be followed in such matters.'

'You might have procedures but I have my pride and going voluntarily into a police station is not on my list of high priorities. It ranks low in my pride league table.'

'If you want to report a crime, you'll have to bend your rules, Claude, and if it's something serious then you'll need our expertise and help – and it won't cost you a penny.'

'Now there's an offer I can't refuse, summat for nowt. I never thought of it like that. All right, if it means getting the full crime detection works without costing me a penny then I'll break the rules of a lifetime. So where do I go?'

'Follow me.'

I led him into the dark corridor from the car park and down two flights of steps before arriving at the inquiry office. As I approached, I could see PC Alf Ventress at the counter working on some kind of register, with Sergeant Blaketon busy in the background.

'Ah, Sergeant,' I said. 'I've brought a customer for you, he wishes to report a crime.'

'Well, that's what we are here for. Where is he?'

'Here, Blaketon,' snapped Claude, poking his head through the hatch. 'And I demand the very best service from you and your officers.'

'We always give our best to special customers, Claude, and that includes you. Have you come to confess to a crime or something?'

'No, I have not! That's the second time I've been asked that question in the last two minutes. It's not funny. I am the *victim* of a crime and don't like having my property stolen so I want it sorting out and detecting which is why I am here. Young Rhea says I have to report it to you.'

'That's the procedure. It is reported here and if we think it requires the special skills of the CID, we will refer it upstairs.'

'Then I might deal with it,' I butted in. 'So I'll go and leave you fellows to sort it out.'

'No, you won't, Rhea,' barked Blaketon. 'You don't bring disreputable characters like Greengrass into this police station and leave somebody else to sort out the mess. You stay here until we've found out what Greengrass really wants. And make sure he doesn't spirit anything away without permission. I'd hate to lose the typewriter.'

'That's uncalled for!' snapped Claude. 'I am not a common thief.'

'But I'm a very experienced police officer, Claude—'

'I want justice, Blaketon,' he interrupted. 'Good old-fashioned English justice along with service from you.'

I butted in to try and bring a halt to the slanging match, saying, 'Claude wants to report a crime, Sergeant.'

'All right, Claude. It can happen to anyone, even you. Let me get a crime report form and then you and I can complete it. It needs to be done before we proceed further. Do you want to come around and into the office, where I can offer you a chair whilst we complete the preliminaries?'

'Now that's what I do call service! A chair! So do I get a cup of tea as well?' Claude left the hatch to enter via a door at the end of the passage. Blaketon ignored the cup of tea comment and found a high stool. He asked Claude to sit upon it at the high counter to complete the form.

'Name and address,' began Blaketon.

'You know all that, there's no need for me to repeat it, is there?'

Blaketon wrote down the details, then asked, 'Date of birth, Claude.'

'Date of birth? What's my birthday got to do with reporting a load of stolen scrap? You'll be wanting to know my occupation next.'

'Born 29 February 1900,' said Blaketon.

'I'm not as old as that!'

'If you won't tell me, I shall have to make an estimate based on your appearance and demeanour,' said Blaketon. 'And so I have made an estimate. And I shall record your occupation as scrap merchant.'

'I'm not a scrap merchant, Blaketon, I am a general dealer of great repute.'

'All right, general dealer it is. Now, when did the crime occur?'

'Last night.'

'What time?'

'Between about half seven last evening and half eight this morning.'

'Overnight then?'

'By Jove, Blaketon, you're as quick as lightning. Yes, it was overnight.'

'Location of crime?'

'Strensford shipyard.'

'The shipyard? What was your old truck doing at the shipyard at night? It's a secure place, Claude, the gates are locked overnight and there's a patrol to stop trespassers and vandals. So how did you bypass that tight security?'

'I didn't bypass anything, I got permission to leave it there. It was loaded when I left it but overnight somebody has nicked my load of precious metal. I call that a crime.'

'Precious metal?'

'It was precious to me; there was a month's wages riding on that truckload when I left it, and now it's gone.'

'I prefer to call it scrap. How much was it worth?'

'I've no idea, I won't have any idea until I sell it but now I can't sell it so I can't give you a value, can I?'

'I need to know the value so I can complete this form.'

'It seems to me that filling in useless forms is more important than getting off your backside and finding the rogue who's nicked my metal! You should be looking for it, not filling forms in. It could be anywhere by now, heading across the sea to Holland or somewhere.'

'You are not being very co-operative, Claude.'

'I always shop there, Blaketon. I'm very co-operative.'

'Is that supposed to be a joke? If you let me get this form

filled in, we can take the next step. But I do need a value, Claude – it's for our crime statistics so that at the end of the year, we can notify the government of the value of property stolen in Strensford and district.'

'And if you happen to find it, do you cross it off your list?'

'Our records will be amended and we will include the value of the recovered property.'

'I'm surprised you blokes recover anything! You take more notice of figures and profit margins than you do of poor victimized people like me suffering from the traumatic effects of crime. So what are you going to do about it?'

'I still need a value.'

'I've said I don't know.'

'I'll estimate it as worth sixty-five pounds.'

'Sixty-five? You could do better than that! It means everything to me!'

'All right. Sixty-six. And that's final unless you tell me more, but in the meantime we shall investigate it, you can be sure about that. We will keep you informed of progress and will let you know the result, if any. Now, one other important matter – can you identify the stolen metal?'

'Identify it? It's just a lorry load of scrap ...'

'But if we catch a criminal in possession of a lorry load of scrap, we must be able to prove whether it's yours or not.'

'Well, I haven't painted my name on all the bits and pieces, if that's what you mean.'

'That's just what I mean. Or some other form of identification.'

'So even if you find my missing scrap, you're saying you'll not believe it's mine unless I can prove it beyond doubt.'

'Got it in one, Claude.'

'Then this has been a waste of time, hasn't it? You could have been out there looking for my stuff instead of sitting here asking daft questions and filling forms in.'

'And you could have helped by making your precious metal easily identified in case of theft.'

I decided to say my piece now and addressed my remarks to Sergeant Blaketon.

'Sergeant, can I make a suggestion? Claude is here with his truck and I am able to visit the shipyard now. So suppose Claude takes me along there, I can search the scene in case his property is still there, and by visiting the scene I might learn more about this incident.'

'That makes sense to me. And it will get Greengrass out of this office!'

'Claude,' I asked, 'have you time to run me to the shipyard so I can visit the scene and make a few inquiries?'

'Now we're getting somewhere. Right, come with me.'

In Claude's rattling old truck, we chugged through the narrow streets and eventually he passed through the shipyard gates where his vehicle was recognized. He was waved through. He drove to the yard where a large pile of scrap towered above the vehicle.

'This is where I loaded up, Detective Rhea, and I left my truck overnight.'

'Why did you do that? You don't usually leave it there, do you?'

'No, it was the first time. I had an invitation, you see, to a birthday party, one of the chaps who helps me load and unload here. It was at the Crab and Lobster down the pier, and he said I could leave the truck here all night and he would find a bed for me. So I did. I loaded up here, then went off with him when he'd finished his shift, and stayed there till this morning. But when the gates opened and I went in, my wagon was empty. Somebody had nicked the lot.'

'From a shipyard that's locked at night?'

'Right! That shows how serious it is. There's a night shift on duty but the gates are closed against the general public. You can get in by ringing a bell and proving who you are and why you want to go in.'

'Right.' I indicated a pile of scrap. 'That huge pile of scrap, is it from your truck?'

'Not all that, no. That's where I loaded up yesterday.'

'Claude, I think word did not get around the staff that you had permission to park here overnight. They thought you'd come to deliver a load of scrap. There are other sites affiliated to this yard, aren't there?'

'Yes, stuff does get dumped here for other scrap dealers to come and take it away ...'

'But you don't recognize any of this?'

'Not a hope. You might be right, Constable Detective Rhea, because the day staff isn't the same as the night staff.'

'So we will never know whether you were robbed of your load or whether it was returned to the pile you took it from to await a truck today.'

'Well, here I am. Does it mean I start all over again?'

And so it transpired. When I made inquiries at the yard's office, I learned that from time to time authorized trucks from their other sites arrived during the night to drop off scrap metal for later collection from the Strensford shipyard.

We never did find out what really happened to Claude's pile of scrap but I managed to get his report written off as 'no crime'. I did think about recording it as lost property but decided against it. I didn't want Sergeant Blaketon quizzing me as to whether Claude had been carrying an insecure load.

CHAPTER 18

AMONG SOME MEMBERS of the Great British Public there was a strong belief that if something had been provided by, say, the town council or the county council, then it belonged to everyone. They believed that public ownership meant that all and sundry owned a share which, in the minds of some, indicated that anyone could take it home as their own property. Examples ranged from 'No Parking' bollards and waste bins in the streets to name signs or direction notices erected along our roads and streets. Why anyone would want to steal such things has never been satisfactorily explained but they rarely reappeared.

It became known to the police that a driver would halt his vehicle close to a litter bin and surreptitiously lift it into the boot to take home as some kind of trophy for use in the garden or even the house. I believe some metal waste bins made excellent incinerators for garden waste and unwanted paper.

The thieves did not regard their actions as theft on the grounds that payment of their rates had helped to purchase the object in question. They seemed to think they were part owners and therefore entitled to take it away and use it for private purposes. They were unaware that the Larceny Act of 1916, then in force, made provision for such erroneous beliefs.

To be honest, however, there were few prosecutions simply

because the disappearance of such bins or signs was rarely reported to the police as a crime. In some cases, I doubt the absence was noticed at all. Such disappearances that were reported could be corrected by councils simply by replacing the missing sign or bin. In the absence of any formal notification of a crime (or *complaint* as it was known), the police did not take action.

I recall visiting a girls' private school near Strensford during some inquiries about shoplifting of make-up and perfumes by its pupils. When I was shown into the headteacher's office, the space on the wall behind her desk was filled with one of those large signs that are bolted to stone bases to announce the name of the town or village. In this case it said CAMBRIDGE.

I had no idea whether it had been stolen from the roadside or whether it was a mocked-up example of such a sign. Indeed, such signs were regularly on sale in tourist areas – SCARBOROUGH was such a sign that was sold in souvenir shops – so I asked the teacher, 'Are you from Cambridge?'

'No, but I was at the university,' she told me. 'My boyfriend at the time managed to obtain that sign for me, as a memento. I've no idea where he got it from.'

'A souvenir shop, I expect,' was my diplomatic answer.

The desire to take home a souvenir of some kind seems particularly strong among tourists. The seaside resorts along our coastline have realized this with shops doing a roaring trade in cheap souvenirs of a trip to Bridlington, Scarborough and elsewhere; they are the sort of trophies which, when you get them home, you wonder why on earth you bought the object and then can't find anywhere sensible to put it.

Sadly, some tourists turn to theft as a means of collecting souvenirs. A friend opened a coffee shop in York, and it was nicely equipped with good-quality fittings and cutlery. Within a week, a hundred teaspoons had been stolen and, being anxious to create the right atmosphere, he replaced them with another hundred – and they were all stolen. Luckily he did not inform the police: if he had done so, our crime figures would, in a very short time, have soared by 200 undetected crimes – and there was very little chance of any of those crimes being detected. However, he did mention it to me because I was then teaching young policemen both criminal law and police procedure, and at break time we all adjourned to his coffee shop. He sought our advice on how to protect his property.

'Buy plastic spoons,' was our advice.

Hotels and inns are among the most vulnerable from thieves. Another friend opened a highly successful village inn and furnished it with portraits of racing horses and models of famous winners of classics like Royal Ascot, the Derby or the Ebor Handicap. One such figure, which stood in the entrance on a high shelf, was stolen and never traced.

Only weeks before settling down to write these notes, my wife and I stayed in a hotel in Suffolk with long sea views from our room. In the room was a handsome pair of binoculars for our use and when I thanked the proprietor for that generous thought, I asked if they were ever stolen. He smiled and said they were sometimes removed without authority but in all cases he wrote to the departed guests whereupon they apologized by saying their husband/wife had packed them, thinking they were their own belongings. Many souvenirs are stolen from hotels, towels being most popular, and I knew of one hotel where a large oil painting had been spirited out by some guests.

Stealing souvenirs is a crime. It is theft and it carries a maximum penalty of ten years' imprisonment – a heavy penalty for nicking a teaspoon!

However, back to street signs. Officers were aware of what was almost a cult practice among some youngsters, with a surprisingly large number removing such signs as souvenirs and mementos of their presence in happy and interesting places. Seldom did they regard their activities as crimes or theft, or even dishonest. It was just a bit of fun.

Long ago, when I was a teenager, I visited the home of a friend who was a keen cyclist and he seemed to have visited every place of consequence in the British Isles. He was proud of his achievements and to celebrate had drawn a large map of the British Isles on a blank wall of his bedroom. And on it were fixed miniature name plates of places he had visited – clearly these were too small to have been used as real directional signs and I assumed he had either bought them in souvenir shops or perhaps taken photographs of the actual signs. On one of my visits, he showed me EDINBURGH, KESWICK, AMBLESIDE, SKIPTON, HARROGATE, RIPON, WHITBY, SCARBOROUGH, YORK and lots more, identifying towns, villages and even stately homes. He had one for CASTLE HOWARD but I had no reason to think his signs were stolen. Such signs could be acquired whenever they were either updated or replaced. In other words, a person with such a collection is not necessarily a thief.

Most who collected such signs seemed to be students at university or college. I got the feeling it was a kind of infectious idea believed to be a good one at the time, especially having drunk a few pints. There seemed to be a contest to see who could collect the largest number, or the most varied. Britain's longest village name, Sutton-under-Whitestonecliffe near Thirsk in North Yorkshire, was displayed on the approaches to the village and it became a collector's item, as indeed was the famous Welsh village sign of Llanfairpg, which was the shortened version of Llanfairpwllgwyngyllgogerychwyrndrobwllllantysiliogogogoch. Translated into English, it means 'St Mary's Church by the pool of the white hazel trees near the rapid whirlpool by the red cave of the Church of St Tysilio'. Britain's shortest name is the village of Ae in Scotland, surely a candidate for stolen name signs, and there is another, Oa, on the island of Islay.

Another trend was to concentrate on castles. Perhaps not surprisingly during my police work I came across a fanatic who collected, or probably stole, the name signs of castles with royal connections. He did not restrict himself to the north of England but operated throughout the whole of Britain. If the castle itself did not have a name plate outside, he would unscrew roadside direction signs from signposts nearby and hoard those in his collection.

There are lots of towns and villages in England which feature 'castle' as part of their name, sometimes as a prefix and sometimes as a suffix. For example, there are five 'Castletons' in the British Isles and a dozen 'Castletowns', and almost seventy further place names that begin with the word 'castle'. Then there are those that end with 'castle': Newcastle comes to mind, being situated within my part of north-east England, while others such as Boscastle and the three Oldcastles (not to mention Old Castleton) were far from my place of work so I did not include them as part of my unofficial survey.

However, the thief researched the history of castles throughout Britain and set about collecting a sign for every one that boasted a royal link. As the crime reports for such thefts were not circulated nationwide, we never knew, with any certainty, the extent of his pilfering.

It was by chance that I gained access to his garage because someone had broken in and stolen his expensive tourist bicycle. While there I noticed the array of 'castle' signs bolted to the walls.

When I asked him where they had come from, he said, 'I collect them, it's my hobby. All have links with royalty and I have permission from the castles or local authorities concerned to take these away: they were all being renewed at the time.'

He showed me some of his prize acquisitions such as a Windsor Castle sign, perhaps our best-known royal residence, and Caernarvon Castle, setting for the 1969 investiture of HRH Prince Charles as Prince of Wales. Edinburgh Castle was featured in his collection, with its strong links with the royal families and history of both Scotland and England. In addition I was surprised to see lesser-known castles such as Danby in the North Riding, which is said to have been the home of one of the wives of Henry VIII, Catherine Parr, and Whorlton Castle near Stokesley, which once belonged to Henry VIII. When we checked with the appropriate authorities, they all replied that they had no record of any signs being stolen, so we could not prosecute anyone for theft.

During World War II, all directional and name signs for towns and villages were removed so as to confuse the enemy and so we had to find our way around without really knowing where we were going. Asking a local stalwart for the name of a town or village, or directions to a particular place, was not always successful because such citizens often regarded strangers as enemy agents. They would either shake their heads or pretend they had no idea, although some would maliciously send visitors in the wrong direction, somehow believing they had thus contributed to the war effort.

CHAPTER 19

Among the range of minor but troublesome crimes was a curious set of circumstances that persisted over several years. The task of dealing with one part of it, but also showing tenderness to its vulnerable victims, was allocated to Detective Constable Shirley Robinson, one of my CID colleagues. Shortly after joining the CID as an aide, I became aware of these crimes when an elderly lady's house at Moulford was broken into. It resulted in a phone call to the CID office at Strensford.

'DC Rhea,' I answered, being alone in the office.

'Is DC Robinson there?' asked a male voice.

'Not at the moment, she's on inquiries in town. Can I help?'

'Just pass on a message when she comes in. Tell her we're investigating another one of those raids on pensioners' homes. It's at Moulford. I'm DC Milburn from Brantsford. Maybe she will give me a call when it's convenient?'

'I'll tell her,' I responded and Milburn rang off without any further explanation, clearly thinking I knew something about such a case or any linked cases. I was not familiar with them because Brantsford was not part of our division.

I gave no more thought to the call until Shirley returned to the office. With some nine years' service, she had been in CID for the past four years or so. A pleasant young woman in her early thirties with black hair and a pleasing manner, she was married to a postal worker and had no children.

Shirley's natural warmth had caused Superintendent 'Arthur' Askey to transfer her to CID. In addition to her normal duties, she had been given special responsibility for children and vulnerable adults who were the victims of crime. At that time, it was regarded as a specialist role to be undertaken by women police officers.

'There was a phone call for you, Shirley,' I told her. 'DC Milburn from Brantsford, he wants you to ring him when it's convenient.'

'Did he say why?'

'He just said it was to do with raids on pensioners' homes.'

'Oh, right. I'll do it now.'

I was completing a file at the other side of the table as she made her call and she was soon jotting down facts and saying things like, 'Not another one ... same old routine ... who's doing all these jobs? It's such a silly thing to do, but frightening for the old folk ...'

When she completed the call, she sighed and looked across to me. 'It's another of those raids on pensioners, Nick. We've got nowhere with them, not a single suspect in the frame and still they keep happening ...'

As if to emphasize her dilemma, she pulled a thick file from the drawer of her filing cabinet and passed it across to me. 'This is the list so far – well over a hundred crimes and not a hint of the identity of the guilty person.'

'I've not come across them,' I admitted. 'They're not all in our divisional area, it seems.'

I glanced quickly at a list of village names in the file, most being within the North Riding of Yorkshire but not in Strensford Division. 'The most recent one was just outside our boundary,' I pointed out.

'It was but most are in our patch, Nick. There are a few in neighbouring forces but not far away so you could say these are all local crimes. The CID offices in neighbouring forces, the East and West Ridings in particular, have been told to ring me if one occurs beyond our force boundaries. As none of the crimes has been committed in urban areas, we haven't established a special contact with York City, Hull or Middlesbrough but I've been delegated to collate details of all the raids. I'm a collator rather than an investigator, but I think the investigating officers are trying to find some kind of pattern or key. So far I've not spotted anything. They all appear to be random attacks.'

'Can you enlighten me? Am I right in thinking they're all raids on pensioners' homes? The caller suggested that.'

'Right, Nick. In all cases, the raider operates during the hours of darkness when the pensioners are in bed. They never hear or see a thing.'

'So how does he, she or they gain entry?'

'By all accounts, he's a slick operator. He opens the kitchen window, usually at the back of the house and out of sight from the street, by slipping a slim-bladed knife through the gap between the woodwork of the top window and the bottom one, and slides open the catch. He never causes damage, but none the less it's classified as a break-in, and as the break-ins are often at night, we treat them as burglaries.'

'So if pensioners are his targets, what's he stealing? They're not generally regarded as wealthy people with money lying around the house or gold-plated dinner plates!'

'Right, but this is the strange thing, Nick. Sometimes it's nothing. He searches the house and then makes his exit, lowering the window after himself so as not to attract attention. He rarely leaves footprints or dirt behind either; he always works on warm, dry nights. There have been times when the householders have reported nothing stolen and then weeks or months later they've noticed something missing – but at that stage it's not easy to link that to the earlier break-in.'

'I can understand that problem.'

'There's another thing to consider. As you know, pensioners do forget where they put things, and often lend things to friends and then forget all about it.'

'That's true enough. So what sort of things is he stealing? In similar crimes, cash is the usual target.'

'Not in this case, Nick. It's very strange but he always takes Coronation mugs. George VI and Elizabeth, May 1937.'

'They're not particularly rare or valuable, are they?' I asked.

'Not especially, there are lots of them around, often in pensioners' homes. Some are in very good condition, without chips or other damage. They're nice mugs, though. Rather short and squat, barrel shaped with a handle and a caption around the lip containing the date. There's a colour picture of the royal couple on the front – George VI and Elizabeth – and their initials are on a blue plaque at the rear. It's known as the Booth Coronation mug. They're popular in America; the Americans love anything connected with our royal family. In all, it amounts to some very puzzling crimes.'

'So chummy thinks they're worth stealing? And taking a risk to get his hands on them? Breaking into houses is always risky.'

'It would seem he's prepared to take that risk. A collection of several mugs in good condition would be worth a few bob in an auction room, I'd say, but not a single item.'

'It's intriguing, Shirley, and I'm not involved in anything right now,' I told her. 'So can I be of any help?'

'I've been keeping records of every theft that's come to our notice but apart from them all involving those mugs and all the victims being pensioners, nothing else stands out. As I said, I've not done much investigating of these crimes, I'm really nothing more than a record keeper, but I haven't had enough time to try and establish any other links between them.'

'One thing does stand out, Shirley. How does the thief know where these pensioners live? How does he know where to find the mugs? If he – or she – is targeting pensioners who own these mugs and not breaking into houses elsewhere, then he must know where to find them. How can he do that if they live in widespread areas? Or are we missing something?'

'I asked my husband – he works for the Post Office – and he thought the burglar must be watching post offices in villages to see which pensioners go in to collect their pensions on a Thursday. And then shadow them on their way home. He waits until dark and they've gone to bed before breaking in.'

'Villages, you say? Are all the attacked premises in villages?'

'Yes, they are. We regard that as significant.'

'It could be very significant, Shirley. You'd not be able to keep such a close eye on pensioners in town because they all disperse in different directions after collecting their pensions from the post office and a lot of them catch buses. You'd lose them in no time.'

'Yes, I'd come to that conclusion. In small villages like those around the moors, it would be fairly easy to follow a pensioner home without him or her realizing, especially if the burglar was dressed like a hiker or was a cyclist. The crook would then attack the house under cover of darkness when everyone was asleep. And remember there are no street lights in most of the villages.'

'Have you any evidence to support those ideas?'

'Just a little. At one of the post offices in a village that had suffered such a raid, I discovered a pensioner had been followed home by a hiker complete with haversack – or rather, the hiker was heading in the same direction as her. He was a stranger, but it might have been a coincidence.'

'And was she burgled later?'

'I think she was but she never realized. She could not tell me if anything had been stolen but did say she'd come downstairs one morning to find the kitchen window catch was open, but the window was closed.'

'And that troubled her?'

'It did. She was sure she'd locked the window when she went to bed; it had been open during the day because it was so hot and she told me she was very security conscious, living alone.'

'Was the hiker ever traced?'

'No, but when I mentioned him at the last meeting we had about this, it appears other villages had been visited by a hiker. One report was of a hiker being seen on pension day, sitting on a bench at the War Memorial, and in another village there was a hiker filling a flask from a pump that is still in working condition. And in both cases, a pensioner's house was burgled that evening and a Coronation mug stolen.'

'Always Thursday evenings? Pension day?' I asked.

'Yes, but we don't know where the hiker spends the time between being spotted during the day and committing the crime late at night.'

'I think, if he was a competent burglar, which he seems to be, he would let himself be seen leaving the village complete with haversack and return later when it was dark. In other words he was establishing an alibi for something that had not yet happened.'

'I can understand that.'

'Have we a description of the hiker?'

'It's fairly vague. Male, fairly tall, wearing hiking gear and hiking boots, carrying a rucksack on his back. Aged in his forties or fifties. Wearing a multi-coloured woollen hat so we don't know the colour of his hair.'

'It's a start. Has that description been circulated?'

'It has, to all local police forces and even to local bus companies and the Post Office investigation division.'

'Any sightings?'

'Sorry, no.'

'All right, Shirley, now another thing. In the cases where nothing was stolen following a night entry, was it because the householders did not collect Coronation mugs?'

'I think so. In one case, the old man of the house thought he'd heard an intruder in the night but couldn't be sure. When he checked, the kitchen window had been opened without breaking the glass – not a difficult thing to do with a sharp knife to unlock it – but nothing had been stolen. And he did not own a Coronation mug.'

'So he'd had a burglar who had found nothing to steal. The raids do appear to be a little dependent on the hit-and-miss system?'

'That's the general feeling. The burglar does not target more than one house at a time. There's at least a week between raids, they're always on Thursdays, and they are in villages a long way from the previously targeted one. He's establishing an alibi of sorts as he goes along.'

'He seems to be a very slippery character. Have you maintained an ongoing list, Shirley, with results?'

'I have.' She opened a file to extract a pad of lined foolscap sheets with a long list of handwritten village names, accompanied by house names, the names of the owner/occupiers, the dates of the raids and whether or not anything had been stolen. It was vividly evident that none of the householders had been physically attacked. In fact, it seems all had slept throughout the raids.

'The villages are all in alphabetical order, Nick,' Shirley pointed out.

'You did well to arrange all those names!' I congratulated her.

'Oh, I didn't do that, Nick. That's how they've been attacked – you'll see the first one begins with A but was also the first in the time scale.'

'Then he *is* meticulous! Methodically going through a list of villages, raiding them one by one, always pensioners and always on Thursdays, pension day. You know, Shirley, if this is his practice, we might be able to forecast where his next visit will be, and then we could keep observations. And we know it will be on a Thursday.'

'One thing to consider, Nick. He doesn't go through all the villages beginning with A. He'll do one from A, the next from B and so on, missing out lots of villages with the same starting letters. For example, he has visited Ainderby but has not yet been to Aislaby, Aldwark, Allerston, Alne, Amotherby, Ampleforth, any of the Appletons, Aske, Askrigg or Aysgarth. He followed Ainderby with a B village. Borrowby in fact.'

'So he has a long way to go in the future and lots of mugs to steal, but he'll be calling at one of those A villages on one of his future rounds.'

'He's reached Moulford now,' she reminded me. 'So his next will begin with letter N.'

I found a road atlas on a shelf in the office and opened it at our part of the North Riding to examine it. 'There are ten villages beginning with N but he won't necessarily raid a house in the first one in alphabetical order, that would be too obvious. So do all the villages that have been raided have both post offices and pensioners? That could be key to his activities – does he raid villages that don't have post offices?'

'Most have one,' she told me. 'Those pensioners without a post office in their own village make use of the one that's nearest. And I'd say most villages have pensioners living there.

He could still shadow them home.'

'It seems we need to establish some kind of undercover operation to watch all the North Riding villages beginning with N next Thursday, especially after dark,' I suggested. 'We need to make use of the village bobbies wherever we can; they'll know the vulnerable people and houses. We also need to use local knowledge and we must find out what our suspect does between watching pensioners leave the post office and carrying out his raids. I don't think he'll spend time in the pub or sitting on a bench, he'd be too conspicuous.'

With the co-operation of Superintendent Askey and the senior uniformed officers of Strensford plus the hierarchy of the CID both locally and in other areas of the North Riding, we made our plans. Fortunately, Shirley and I were included and played a key role. The meeting took a long time with the sessions being spread over two days but eventually a decision was made.

There were twelve villages in the North Riding whose names began with N and so they were targeted with special patrols and observations. Of the twelve, three had the same prefix – Nun. Our survey revealed that all had village post offices and all housed considerable numbers of pensioners. The three that prompted our next action were Nunfield, Nunnington and Nunthorpe.

'I doubt if he would use a list,' suggested Shirley. 'If he's using some kind of system to conceal his movements, that would be too obvious a choice. He'd avoid it.'

'In that list –' I felt I should make my own views known '– three begin with the same prefix, Nun. What's the betting he would pick the first of them, making it easy to remember which comes next for a future visit?'

DI Baldwin then entered the fray. 'The short answer is that we have no idea. We're guessing he might visit one post office to follow a pensioner home but might not raid that particular house until sometime in the future, thus divorcing any sightings from the actual break-ins. We're dealing with a clever weirdo here – who in their right mind would go around stealing Coronation mugs? It means he will not behave rationally and so we really can't predict his movements. It's a case of good old-fashioned police work – we patrol as many of the likely locations as we can and if any of us spot the hiker, we shadow him without him knowing – and alert our teams by reporting to base. We will be issued with portable radio sets, courtesy of the RAF police.'

'It seems a lot of bother for a few old mugs,' grumbled DC Sherlock Watson.

'They're all crimes of burglary,' retorted Baldwin. 'One of our most serious criminal offences and more so if vulnerable people are being systematically targeted. We must work together to catch him, preferably in the act if possible.'

And so, on the following Thursday morning in all North Riding villages with names beginning with the letter N, undercover patrols were at work. They were pretending to be artists, hikers, bird-watchers, flower experts, surveyors and a host of other working people or tourists who might routinely visit small villages.

I was pleased that it was Shirley who spotted a hiker emerging from the village post office at Nunfield. He was clutching a book of stamps as he began to follow a small aged lady, albeit keeping a long distance behind. Shirley, pushing her three-month-old niece in a pram, alerted us all and said she was shadowing him. The lady went to Lilac Cottage behind the church, unlocked her door and went in; the hiker walked past with Shirley and pram several yards away, but then he turned down a narrow lane which returned him to the village green. It seemed he had found his target so Shirley tailed him with great care and saw him enter a field where he disappeared into a small tent. Now we knew how he whiled away the time – he had brought his own hiding place – but we decided we could not maintain a vigil in case he noticed us.

Shirley was able to provide a general description which matched the one already in our possession. The only way forward was to set a trap that night at Lilac Cottage; if he did not appear, the cottage would be supervised the next Thursday, and the following Thursdays if that proved necessary. Once he was arrested, we could establish his identity and search his home in an attempt to understand why he was stealing 1937 Coronation mugs.

To cut short a long story, the operation was successful. Shirley and a uniformed police officer sat in the darkness of Lilac Cottage with the widowed Mrs Ada Hird, aged eighty-two, who, after being fully informed about the event, wanted to remain awake to enjoy the fun as she called it. She owned a Coronation mug from 1937, and showed the team the shelf upon which it stood in the living room.

It was not a long wait: at 1.30 a.m. they heard faint noises coming from the kitchen as chummy was prising open the window, then saw torchlight moving as he made his way into the other parts of the house. The reception team did not try to prevent him or arrest him too early – they sat motionless in the dark, wanting to catch him in possession of the mug and so provide the evidence necessary for an arrest and conviction. He was caught in the act – red-handed, as the saying goes – and taken to Strensford Police Station for due process of the law.

His name was Cyril Dunn, an otherwise harmless eccentric who lived alone in the small town of Galtreford, where he was receiving help for his mental problems.

He possessed an encyclopaedic knowledge of the North Riding because he read all the topographic books and magazines.

When his tiny rented cottage – the former home of his deceased parents – was searched, the spare bedroom was full of Coronation mugs, not upon shelves but spread about the spare bed, the window ledges, the wardrobes and the floor. Clearly, he had a 'thing' about them.

DI Baldwin asked, 'Why did you steal these mugs, Cyril?'

'Because I've always wanted one,' he said quietly, head down and staring at the floor.

'You could have had one without going to all this trouble.'

'My mum wouldn't let me have one, she had one and gave it away so I never got it and because I wanted one I thought there would be lots of old men and women who had them and didn't really want them but when I called and asked them, they told me to go away … so I thought I would help myself. Once I got one, I wanted another.' And then he started to weep. Shirley went to comfort him.

Cyril appeared before Strensford Magistrates' Court, who decided he was not fit to enter a plea and he was ordered to be detained in a suitable mental establishment for treatment and care. The court ordered that the mugs in his possession should, where possible, be returned to their true owners – but very few wanted them back.

As one lady said, 'It's allus been up there gathering dust, I'm pleased to see t'back of it. It was my husband's really and nobody wanted it when he died.'

The unwanted mugs were sold for charity.

CHAPTER 20

'THIS IS ONE for you, Nick. Shirley's out on another job and might be a long time so can you deal with this young lady?' Detective Sergeant Latimer had brought her into the CID room we used as our office. 'She reported to uniform downstairs but Sergeant Blaketon in his wisdom felt this is a case for us.'

A rather slender young woman with long, straight jet-black hair and a pale face stood before us; she looked to be around seventeen or eighteen years old. She wore sandshoes, a grey skirt and a blue jerkin-style top and I could see she was either nervous or embarrassed.

'Of course, Sergeant.' I smiled in an effort to make our visitor feel more at ease and led her to the table I shared with the other Ds. I indicated a chair and invited her to be seated.

'I'm Detective Constable Rhea,' I introduced myself. 'So what's your name?'

'Jenny Forbes,' she replied. 'I live on the council estate on East Side. Number 17 Harbour Rise.'

'I know it.' I nodded, refraining from commenting on the social problems of that district. 'So how can I help?'

Looking as if she didn't really want to be there, she licked her thin lips and wrung her hands as they rested on her lap, then whispered, 'I really wanted to talk to a police lady.'

'There isn't one here just now,' I apologized. 'And DC Shirley Robinson is out on a job and might be a long time. If it's urgent and troubling you, I could always ask our secretary to talk to you or we could arrange for you to come back at a suitable time when we have a female officer available.'

'Oh no, I don't really want to be a nuisance ...'

'I am a man of the world,' I told her with all the authority of a 22-year-old. 'And I have a girlfriend, a sister and lots of girl cousins. You needn't be shy. Do you work in town?'

'Yes, at Strensford Tailors, the clothing factory. I'm in my break time.'

'So are you here to report a crime?'

She produced a thin smile and nodded, saying, 'Well, I hope you're not going to be embarrassed ...'

'Police officers don't get embarrassed.' I tried to be confident as I wondered what was troubling her. 'We're expected to deal with all kinds of situations involving men, women and children, and we are trained to be discreet.'

I wondered if she had been raped or assaulted; lots of such victims did find it difficult speaking to a police officer – male or female.

After another thin smile and more wringing of her hands, she said, 'Somebody is stealing my underwear. Off the clothes line.'

'Sadly, that is a fairly common problem, Jenny. Lots of towns and villages suffer from strange men who steal underwear for reasons best known to themselves. Has it been going on for very long?'

'Not really. A week or two. At first I thought the wind was blowing them off the line – we do live in a very windy place – but now I think someone is stealing them.'

'Exactly what are they taking?'

'My knickers.' She blushed and lowered her gaze. 'Eight or nine pairs have gone … it's costing me a fortune.'

'No bras?'

'No, he's not touched those. Just knickers.'

'Have your neighbours or others lost any? Or other items of washing?'

She shook her head. 'I don't think so, no one mentioned anything being taken.'

'So what's special about yours? Have you a secret admirer? Someone who might have been pestering you, someone at work or someone you might have met socially …'

'I have a boyfriend, he works at the factory as well, but it's not him. I asked and he laughed and said no.'

'So you think it's someone unknown to you?'

'Yes, my things disappear during the daytime when I'm at work. Dad's out at work as well and my older brother is; Mum hasn't a job and is in a lot but goes out shopping and things, visiting friends … so the place can be empty during weekdays.'

'Why would anybody steal your underwear, Jenny?'

'They're frillies.'

'Frillies?'

'Like that tennis player used to wear when I was little. Gorgeous Gussy.'

'Oh, I remember. My dad used to go on about her. She didn't become famous because of her tennis but because of her frilly pants!'

'Yes, my dad was the same. He went on about them. He always watched Gussy on telly; Mum didn't like that. I don't know what it is about frilly panties …'

'Yet you wear them?' I smiled.

'I like them,' was all she volunteered. 'But I need the thieving to stop. He's costing me a fortune is that knicker-pincher.'

'I need to know how many pairs have been stolen, their

makes and colours, what makes them distinctive, and how much they are worth.'

She provided the information They were various colours – red, purple, light blue and white – but all had frills. She thought eight or nine pairs had been stolen but didn't think they'd be worth more than £3 for the lot.

I noted the details on the crime complaint form and then asked if her parents would object to a detective concealing himself or herself in her home to keep watch. She wasn't sure about that because her mother did not like her wearing such provocative panties. Alternatively, I suggested we could use a plain car parked in a suitable position to supervise the washing line. Jenny seemed happy with that plan. I made the point that if the thief realized his activities had been reported to the police, he would probably end his stealing. Peace would again reign on Harbour Rise. Jenny smiled her thanks.

'Are you on the phone at home?' I asked. 'Is your mum at home most of the day?'

'Yes, but quite often there's no one in to answer it. Mum is very busy, she looks after old folk.'

'That's good of her. I'll need to contact either you or her if we catch the thief and you'll be asked to identify the recovered property. Can we contact you on the phone at work?'

'No, but there's a kiosk at work for the staff; we can make outgoing calls and take incoming ones if they're urgent. We do them in our break times.' At my request she wrote the number on a slip of paper.

'So you'd rather I didn't contact your mum?' I put to her.

'Right. She doesn't know I'm here and wouldn't want the police going to our house. The neighbours talk, you know, that estate's a weird place to live. I hope to get my own place when I've got a bit put by, me and my fella. I've had enough of living on an estate like that.'

'It's good to be ambitious, so I wish you the best of luck, Jenny.'

I explained that I would make discreet inquiries around Harbour Rise without mentioning her name or address, my purpose being to see whether anyone else had suffered such losses but also to check whether or not a pervert was living nearby or within striking distance. Some alert resident might have noticed the thief prowling around the gardens and backyards, and I explained I would check our own sources of information to trace such individuals. As a departing gesture I asked Jenny to let me know if any of the stolen items turned up – that did happen sometimes, with messages or worse among the frillies.

As a crime had been reported, I had to visit the scene but decided that a low-profile approach would be wise. I went to see Sergeant Kilner in the admin office to ask if he had a supply of crime prevention leaflets I could use to justify my presence on Harbour Rise. Having not found any such suspect weirdoes in our system, certainly none living on or near Harbour Rise, I caught a bus that would deliver me to the estate, making sure I kept the ticket to claim my expenses!

Once there, I began a tour of the streets as I pushed the leaflets through letterboxes. I could feel eyes watching me. It was a bleak place with unkempt gardens, rubbish on what should be the lawn area, litter in the streets, including empty bottles along with discarded fish-and-chip papers, and much else besides. Broken-down cars, old bikes and children's trikes were left to rust because no one could deal with them.

'Something going on?' asked a large and fierce-looking middle-aged woman who was clearly anxious to establish the purpose of my presence. I wondered if she was a self-appointed guardian of the estate – certainly she exuded that kind of image.

From my viewpoint, I realized she might be able to help me.

She was standing at her front door at number 19 with her arms folded in what looked like an act of defiance. 'A party somewhere? Are we doing something we shouldn't? Are you from the council? Or are you selling encyclopaedias? Is it somebody to vote for in the next election?'

'Nothing like that, I'm a detective, and this is our latest crime prevention advice. We're asking people to take care with their homes and belongings, lock doors and windows of houses and cars especially at night, that sort of thing.'

'Well, I wouldn't trust anybody who lives on this estate,' she said. 'Light-fingered bunch that they are. You can't leave anything in the garden at night, it'll be gone next morning.'

'Such as?' I asked, anxious to keep her talking so I could learn as much as possible about this place. She appeared increasingly willing to talk to me.

'Kids' toys mainly, trikes, beach balls … you name it, they'll nick it.'

'What about stuff left on washing lines? Sheets and so on.'

'Not in the daytime, mister. Too many eyes watching from behind lace curtains, but at night, well, anything goes. You never leave stuff out at night, unless you want rid of it. We women always fetch the washing in at night. Sheets are worth a lot, and pillowcases. But I've known folks leave stuff outside their front door when they want rid of it – somebody will think it's worth nicking, it will get taken away, you can be sure of that.'

'Maybe our crime prevention people should concentrate on night time?' I was keen to keep the conversation moving ahead.

'That or else have bobbies patrolling the estate at night, all night.'

'Right. We do have officers patrolling the whole town at night,' I stressed.

'Mebbe so, but you'll never stop crime in these places, young man, it's a way of life.'

'Do you get burglaries then?'

'No, none of us have stuff worth pinching by burglars, it's not worth the risk breaking in; it's stuff left outside at night that gets stolen.'

'Not even a weirdo pinching knickers?'

'Not in the daytime, young man, I could guarantee that. As I said, too many eyes watching from behind lace curtains. If there was somebody pinching stuff from our washing lines, we'd all get together to make sure we nobbled him. We wouldn't stand by and watch it happen, and when us women from this estate gather in a mob, he'd stand no chance. He'd wish he'd never done it, I can tell you. I'd even say he would put his manhood at risk, if you follow me.'

'So there's no weirdo pinching frilly knickers from these houses?' I decided to put a direct question.

'Do you mean from that Forbes lass at number seventeen? My neighbour?'

'I wasn't thinking of her in particular, but we've had reports from other places.' I told a white lie to protect Jenny. 'Apparently, in some areas, the stealing of women's underwear from washing lines is very common, both in the daytime and at night.'

'Not here it isn't. As I said, we watch our belongings. It goes with the life we live here: watch it or lose it, we say. So when we put our washing out, there's always one of us watching; nothing organized, you understand, just good neighbours, especially if one of us has to go to the shops and leave washing drying on the line.'

'It sounds very neighbourly to me.' I was now beginning to understand something of life on this estate. 'Very commendable.'

'Well, I reckon we could give your bosses some useful advice about crime prevention,' she said, adding mischievously, 'but if that Forbes lass has been reporting knicker thieves, it's not that. It's just her mum taking 'em off the line to save embarrassment.'

'Embarrassment?' I frowned at her.

'Well, mebbe I shouldn't tell you this, but I can see you are an honourable young man. It was Mr Forbes, you see, Jenny's dad. He couldn't take his eyes off Gorgeous Gussy when she was playing tennis in her fancy pants and it annoyed his missus, who'd never let herself be seen dead in such things. So can you imagine how she felt when young Jenny started wearing the same things in different colours? Well, she couldn't abide it when Jenny hung 'em out to dry on her washing line in full view so now Mrs Forbes makes sure nobody sees 'em.'

'So what does she do with them?'

'Now you'll have to ask her yourself. I don't know and if you talk to her you never spoke to me, right? I don't want to be labelled as an old nosey Miss Tittle-Tattle.'

'I think I'd better speak to Jenny. Maybe she can come up with a solution. So do you think her mother has thrown Jenny's frillies out?'

'No, she's too careful with money to do that! They'll be hidden in the house, I reckon.'

'I'll have words with Jenny when she comes out of the factory after work,' I said. 'Can I tell her who told me all this?'

'No, you can't! I don't want to get labelled as a copper's nark but I do want to get this sorted out. I wouldn't want my friend Mrs Forbes being arrested as a knicker-pincher, would I?'

'Well, thanks for all this.' I could now write this off as 'no crime' but first I had to break the news to Jenny.

CHAPTER 21

DURING THOSE EARLY days with the CID, I began to realize the true extent of what might be termed petty crime. By that I include those minor crimes which do not cause physical injury or a great loss to anyone and which do not entail breaking into property such as houses, shops, stores and garages. Likewise my understanding of petty crime does not include the theft of large expensive objects like motor vehicles, yachts or steam engines, or dishonesty involving the stealing or misappropriation of huge sums of money whether by deceit, forgery or violence.

I would probably not include the theft of bridges, either, which did happen from time to time. I remember one occasion when thieves got away with an entire wooden footbridge from a public park and another when an iron road bridge was spirited away even though it carried a main road across a busy river. People thought the night-operating 'workmen' were genuine.

Petty crime is not a legal definition but one of convenience, and my own personal view is that it includes countless means of committing small-time crime such as stealing sweets from shop counters, taking plants from roadside gardens, helping oneself to goods thrown out for the dustmen to collect, stealing fruit and vegetables on display outside shops such as a single apple or orange, taking home items of cutlery from restaurants, helping oneself to paper clips from the office or items from hotel bedrooms such as the towels or ornaments on display and, I suppose, finding something valuable that has been lost such as a gold ring, jewellery or watch but deciding to keep it. In religious terms, such unlawful acts are also regarded as sins – the Commandments say, quite simply, 'Thou shalt not steal.' Of interest is the fact that the term 'petty larceny' used to be an offence and it was the stealing of personal property less than a statutory value of £2 but that definition was abolished before I joined the police. However, it continued in name, like petty sessions and petty jury.

Experience has shown me that many people do not report the theft of small, invaluable items – although once, when I became the village constable at Aidensfield, I had to deal with a farmer who reported the theft of a short length of rope. It was about a yard long, as thick as a human finger and it had a loop at each end. When I responded to his call, I had to inspect the scene of the crime, a vital element of any such investigation.

As the farmer, named Sid, stood and stared at the blank and empty wall of his cattle byre, he explained that he hung the rope on the outside wall where it was easily located when he wanted to use it. He believed it was a passer-by who had stolen it, but for what purpose neither he nor I could guess.

Had someone removed it because it would make a useful tow rope for a small broken-down car, or was it wanted to help carry something heavy by lashing it to the frame of a pedal cycle or the panniers of a motorbike? Or perhaps it was required as a dog lead? Or to hold up a workman's trousers? Or to move a bull or horse somewhere? Help to lash down the lid of an overfull suitcase, perhaps? I could think of many uses for a short piece of strong rope with loops at each end.

In recording the theft of the rope in my pocket book, I was

reminded of a very careful lady I knew. She saved pieces of string and had divisions in the kitchen drawers for each length. The entire area of that drawer was labelled 'pieces of string', with one section labelled 'very long pieces' and another saying 'long enough to go round pans', another 'about right for jam jars' while a smaller drawer said 'short enough to tie around a finger to make me remember things' – but the one I liked best contained very short cut-off pieces and was labelled 'pieces of string with no further use'.

As I recorded the details, I realized that when I submitted the necessary crime report my superiors would question my wisdom in treating this as a crime. At that time some police forces had ceased to record crimes where the stolen goods were valued at less than £5.

My force had not taken that step and so I went ahead with my investigation.

'Can you put a value on this bit of rope?' I asked Sid. 'I need it for my crime report.'

'It's worth nowt money-wise.' He was a dour Yorkshire farmer of some sixty-five years, with a few days' growth of beard and the eternal whiff of cow muck about him. 'But for me it's priceless.'

'Why's that?'

'I'm a one-man business, Mr Rhea, and can't afford to pay for help so I depend on that bit o' rope.'

'How?'

'Well, you see yon gate?' He indicated one that led into a passing lane. 'My milking herd's in yon hundred-acre field down t'lane and I have to drive 'em up t'lane for milking here in t'shippen. But I need t'gate to be open when they're heading this way, otherwise they'll keep marching on and get on to t'main road. Now t'gate won't stand open by itself, Mr Rhea, because it's on a slight slope, so before I start herding 'em, I have to tie it back on a big hook with that bit o' rope. It's just t'right length, perfect for t'job. Without it, Mr Rhea, I'd never get my cows milked, so mebbe you could put a value on that!'

'I take your point, Sid, and thanks. I'll record it as being worth five bob and will ask around in the hope I can find it.'

'I'd appreciate that, Mr Rhea.'

'Can you be sure it's not on your premises? Have you looked? You've not put it somewhere and forgotten about it?'

'Searched high and low, Mr Rhea, it's nowhere to be seen. It's been nicked, all right. I'll guarantee that.'

And so, despite some laughter and much sarcasm from Sergeant Blaketon, whose task was to forward my crime report to higher authority, Sid's rope was officially recorded as stolen despite Alf Ventress saying it wasn't long enough to hang a horse thief.

Whatever officialdom's view on my report, it was my duty to make inquiries in an effort to recover it. I was duty-bound to find the thief so I decided to ask Claude Jeremiah Greengrass if he knew anything about it – he travelled a lot, and often visited local farms. A couple of days later, I found him on his ranch at Hagg Bottom, sorting though a pile of what appeared to be rubbish, and explained my mission.

'I'm not accusing you of stealing the rope, Claude, but being a businessman who travels widely, I wondered if you'd come across it.'

'As a matter of fact, Constable Rhea,' he replied, 'I've got it right here but have no idea where it's come from.'

He led me to a large wooden crate which appeared to be full of bits of wire and rope, and sure enough, the short length of rope resting on top looked just like the one described to me by Sid, with a loop at each end.

'So how did it get here?' I asked.

'I saw this chap parked in that small lay-by between

Aidensfield and Elsinby; he was trying to tie up the rear bumper of his old car, it was hanging down and touching the road, rattling along. Anyway, the bit o' rope he was trying to use wasn't long enough and in any case, there was nothing he could fasten it to, so he tossed it away into t'hedgeback. I happened to be passing and stopped because it looked like a bit of good rope to me. He drove off in a rattling and banging rush as I pulled up, but I found the bit o' rope. I've no idea where he got it from but it's no good for me ... too short ... loops at each end ... useless, really.'

I explained Farmer Sid's technique of fastening his gate back with this very piece of rope and thanked Claude, who said he might call on Sid in the hope of getting a gallon of free milk as a reward. I took possession of the rope and returned it to Sid, who was delighted. And I informed Sergeant Blaketon that I had traced the rope but not yet found the thief.

'Don't stop your inquiries, Rhea, a thief is a thief whatever the thing he or she stole. It was the poet Francis Bacon who said, "Opportunity makes a thief."'

'I didn't know you studied the works of the great poets, Sergeant?'

'I don't, it was my old sergeant who told me that, so now I'm telling you so you can make use of it sooner or later.'

'There is one in the Bible, Sergeant. It says, "Woe, woe, woe unto them that draw iniquity with cords of vanity, and sin as it were with a cart rope."'

'I can't argue with that,' he said and walked away, shaking his head.

As the newest aide to CID, I was ordered to investigate a reported crime which some might have regarded as petty, but which the loser of the property considered tantamount to treachery. Someone had stolen one of his garden gnomes; not only that, it was one of Snow White's Seven Dwarfs – Bashful, in fact. And the theft had ruined his line-up of dwarfs.

I was despatched by DS Latimer to investigate the crime because the victim, a Mr Orlando Crump, had dialled 999 and appeared to be very angry and upset at his loss. I went immediately to the scene of the crime at 17 Pottery Lane, a brick-built detached house whose garden and rockery were full of garden gnomes, miniature windmills and small dolls' houses plus a modern arched bridge for toy cars. It all looked very twee among the surrounding conventional houses with their neat lawns, roses and smart gardens.

At first glance as I strode up the path I could not see any gap from where Bashful might have escaped or been kidnapped (gnome-napped, perhaps?) but the garden area looked like a crowd scene at a fancy dress party. I wondered if the owner had made a mistake. Perhaps he had mislaid Bashful? If the little fellow had wandered from his plinth, he could be lost among all the others but they were saying nowt.

I rang the doorbell and a gentleman in carpet slippers and a long Japanese-style of housecoat responded. I wondered if he had just got out of bed. He did not invite me inside. We had our chat on the doorstep.

'I'm Detective Constable Rhea,' I informed him. 'I understand you have reported a theft? I am here to investigate the crime.'

'Ah, good man! Thank you for responding so quickly. Yes, it is Bashful, he is missing from his plinth. He never moves away of his own accord, Officer, so I can only think he has been kidnapped. Heaven knows what might happen to him in the wrong hands.'

'Have you searched among all the others? He might have been mislaid or knocked over by an inquisitive fox or something.'

'There is no sign of him, Officer. I have searched everywhere inside and out, next door's gardens, the dustbin, everywhere. Bashful is not here, I can guarantee that.'

I was making notes in my pocket book as he kept me on the doorstep and then I asked the standard question, 'What is the value of the stolen property?'

'Value, Officer?' and his eyebrows rose. 'How can one place a value on a trusted friend?'

'All right, Mr Crump, what will it cost to replace Bashful?'

'He is irreplaceable, Officer. One cannot obtain individual Bashfuls, they are very hard to find. They come in a set of seven – you are familiar with the Seven Dwarfs, are you?'

'Happy, Sleepy, Doc, Bashful, Sneezy, Grumpy and Dopey,' I responded, to show him I was not completely out of touch with reality.

'Then you will know that Dopey is almost impossible to find outside a complete set and so he is the most expensive to replace. You're probably talking a couple of pounds for a top-quality Dopey. Really good Bashfuls are not so expensive, one pound ten shillings, perhaps, but not easy to find as a solo item. Dealers generally want us to buy full sets.'

'Are they very heavy to move?' I asked. 'I mean, could a child carry one away?'

'There is a space at the rear of the base of each figure, Mr Rhea, for buyers to insert specially designed iron weights. This is to stop them being dislodged by strong winds but a child could tip one on to its back and the weight would slide out. They are then quite portable even for a small child. I'm not sure what they are made from, it's a sort of plastic material but very solid – they won't fracture if they're dropped.'

'And has that happened here?'

'I did not find the weight but I suppose it could have slid out whilst being carried off. I've had no one tell me of its recovery.

And there are two broken pieces lying around.'

'All right, now I need a description of the stolen article. We will circulate it in our stolen property supplements and, of course, we shall make inquiries at all the known dealers. I am not sure of the market for stolen gnomes.'

'I will get you a photograph of Bashful.' Mr Crump vanished inside without inviting me in, and emerged with a black-and-white photograph, which he handed to me.

'I need to know the colours and size,' I told him.

'Oh, about a foot tall with a red pointed hat, a green jacket, dark brown trousers, black shoes ... blue eyes which are downcast and a prominent chin ... very handsome, in fact. But very shy, hence his habit of not looking you in the eye. Oh, and he has pink blushes on his cheeks.'

I noted these details and then asked, 'Do you know of any other incidents where garden gnomes have been taken?'

'I do, as a matter of fact, but no one has reported them to the police. They feel the gnomes will be placed in someone's garden and let's face it, Officer, one gnome is just like any other. It is hardly possible to know which is one's own if they are all mixed up in someone else's garden.'

'Could you identify your Bashful as your own among a crowd?'

'I could indeed, Officer. Mine has a black splodge of paint on the underside, on the sole of each of his shoes; I put them there.'

'That will be a great help if we find Bashful.'

'I do hope you trace him, Officer, he means such a lot to me. I'm going to get very emotional if I stand here talking about him for much longer ... I do miss him ... sorry, but I must go in ...'

'I'll keep in touch and will let you know of any progress,' I called after him, but he was gone and the door was closed.

I began to ask questions in the locality and in fact came

across several houses with gnomes in their gardens but perhaps not so numerous as those of Mr Crump. In one case, a woman was working in her garden and I stopped for a chat. After identifying myself and explaining my purpose, she said, 'Oh yes, several of us have lost our gnomes. One or two seem to disappear here and there, not a large amount.'

'Did anyone inform the police?'

'Oh, I don't think so. It could be children playing pranks although Mr Henderson at number twenty-seven around the corner reckons he saw a huge dog carrying one away not so long ago – in the late evening when it was getting dark.'

'Was it one of Mr Henderson's gnomes?'

'No, he doesn't keep gnomes. I think it belonged to a neighbour. Mr Henderson should be at home now if you want a word – he's retired.'

And off I went to Mr Henderson's smart bungalow at number twenty-seven and found him in the garden. He was a stout man with thick grey hair and I reckoned he was in his late seventies. He was tending one of his borders so I hailed him and introduced myself and my purpose.

'Oh yes, Mr Rhea, I saw that dog. It was huge, as big as a St Bernard, I'd say, except it was all black. Very hard to see at night but I spotted it in the lights of a passing car because it was carrying something. Then I realized it was a garden gnome, I noticed its red pointed hat and brown tunic. Sadly I lost it in the darkness but have no idea who the gnome belonged to – not Mr Crump, though. I saw him in the street and he'd not then lost any of his. But if it's gone now, it could be that dog. Maybe it's got a fetish about gnomes and dwarfs?'

'And the dog? Any idea of its owner?'

'There is a breeder on the edge of town, so I believe. Breeds them and shows them, and they are used as rescue dogs, like St Bernards.'

Mr Henderson did not know the breeder's name and address but I hurried back to the police station where Alf Ventress was on office duty – and he knew everything, an absolute fount of local knowledge.

'Oh yes,' he told me. 'Lane Ends Farm on the Eltering Road. Apart from Newfoundlands, he breeds prize bulls and show cockerels. Nice chap, very successful. He's called Dixon, Harry Dixon of Dixon's Dogs.'

And so I was allowed to borrow the CID car to drive the two miles to visit Mr Dixon as I warmed to the idea of tracing the missing gnome.

Dixon was a loud, excitable character with a large ginger beard and he boomed a welcome as I found him in the fold yard. After explaining my mission, he smiled and said, 'Well, at least I now know where Lucifer finds some of those things. He comes home with all sorts, Mr Rhea: dolls, gnomes, footballs, anything left outside, even cushions and tea cosies. He can open the gate if I forget to lock it so I never know when he's on the forage but I have a barn full of his trophies and don't know their owners. I hope you can help me, I need to get rid of them. Follow me.'

On the way, he explained that twice every year he held open days, which included Lucifer's barn and its collection of souvenirs – it was known as Lucifer's Locker.

Many items were claimed but a substantial number never found their true home and after a suitable interlude were offered to charities. I was allowed in and Mr Dixon showed me the collection of garden gnomes. They and the other items covered the floor of the barn. I examined all the gnomes, of which there were many, then remembered Mr Crump's black marks on the feet, and after a brief search managed to find the missing Bashful.

Lucifer came in and sat beside me as I examined his trophy,

wagging his tail as I said, 'I'm arresting you, Lucifer, for stealing this gnome,' but he didn't appear to care. And so I took it away and restored it to the rightful owner, urging him to ensure his garden gate was closed in case Lucifer went on another of his night-time trophy-gathering expeditions.

I had made my first arrest as a detective, even if it was a dog.

CHAPTER 22

DURING THOSE EARLY days as an aide to the CID, murder was one of the rarest of crimes in the North Riding of Yorkshire. I have no official statistics at hand but from memory there was an average of only one or two cases each year, while city areas were recording double figures. I recall a local case of murder in the 1950s, which was a botched abortion attempt by a so-called back-street abortionist. Her crude work led to the death of a woman. At the subsequent inquest, the coroner recorded a verdict of murder although this was later reduced to a charge of manslaughter due to the lack of 'malice aforethought'.

Illegal abortions were surprisingly frequent with many infringing the Offences Against the Person Act of 1861. The Infant Life (Preservation) Act of 1929 specifically sought to protect the lives of unborn children though there was a legal defence if the death of an unborn child had been necessary to preserve the life of the mother. Abortion in an NHS hospital or other place approved by the Secretary of State was legal if carried out by a registered medical practitioner following the opinion of two such doctors. The relevant statute was the Abortion Act, 1967. Soon afterwards, illegal abortions became a thing of the past.

Without doubt, murders were rare in Strensford and the

district and it was difficult to recall the most recent attempt of either a case of murder or manslaughter. Oddly enough, some bar-room lawyers believed that World War II had led to fewer murders and one apparent reason for this, which I heard being discussed in a pub one evening, was that potential murderers were serving in HM Forces where they were kept fully occupied by killing the enemy. There may have been some truth in that but I've seldom heard war being regarded as a crime prevention technique.

Once the war was over, things returned to normal and reports of murder and mayhem began to reappear. In fact, the following murder case occurred in Strensford while I was serving as a CID aide in the late 1950s.

One procedure I recall from my service as a police cadet some sixty-three years ago (1952) in a nearby market town was that it was occasionally necessary to 'call in The Yard' when cases of murder occurred. This was because many provincial police forces, both urban or rural, lacked the expertise and experience necessary to cope with a complex or long-running murder investigation. To help them identify and prosecute the culprits, highly experienced detectives from New Scotland Yard were called in. This was long before the advent of highly qualified forensic scientists and locally trained CID experts. Each Yard team comprised two detectives who wore long raincoats and trilby hats – not a very effective disguise. They travelled by train and local lodgings were secured for the duration of their inquiry. One was a detective superintendent and his sidekick was a detective sergeant. They lacked modern technology and sophisticated means of communication but on occasions were resented by the local CID. Their arrival suggested the local CID was incapable of solving a murder on its own doorstep.

Calling in The Yard was not compulsory; it was a service provided by New Scotland Yard and was utilized as and when thought necessary by a local chief constable. However, the practice led to some crime writers erroneously believing that Scotland Yard was the headquarters of the English police service. It wasn't, and never has been. By the late 1950s, early 1960s, the provincial police forces in Britain had become quite capable of dealing with serious crime and major incidents and so they bade a grateful farewell to 'Binn of The Yard', as the Met's famous detectives had become known.

During my attachment to the CID, if we received the report of a sudden death which seemed suspicious, there was no question of calling in The Yard. It was our responsibility.

It was a couple of minutes or so past 8.30 one Tuesday morning and I had just arrived at the CID office, looking forward to another day. When the phone rang, it was answered by Detective Sergeant Tom Latimer.

'CID. Latimer,' he responded. It was an internal call from the inquiry office downstairs.

'Blaketon,' announced the duty sergeant. 'We've a report of a body been found, Tom, female, elderly. It was reported as a routine sudden death but following our examination of the scene along with some preliminary inquiries, we feel it is suspicious. I've preserved the scene and suggest your officers be involved. We've a uniform guarding the house in question and the police doctor has been called. The address is 19 Abbey Lea at the far side of the harbour.'

'You've not moved anything?'

'Fortunately, no. I've secured the scene with PC Ventress on duty outside the address; he's dealt with lots of sudden deaths and is reliable. I'm also on my way now. See you there.'

'Before you go, Oscar, who's the deceased?'

'Alice Scott, unmarried and in her seventies.'

'And who informed you?'

'The next-door neighbour, Mrs Jenny Wallace, a woman of

similar age. She has a key for the house.'

'Right, I'm on my way.'

He replaced the handset, turned to me and said, 'A possible suspicious death, Nick, you'd better come with me. You'll find it a useful experience.'

Detective Sergeant Latimer drove carefully through the narrow streets as the town was already busy with staff heading to their offices and workplaces. Early shoppers were thronging the pavements and traffic was building up. Our destination meant crossing the harbour bridge and finding our way to Miss Scott's address among a conglomeration of narrow alleys and steep streets. The eastern side of town, clinging to the cliff side, was like a rabbit warren of old cottages but DS Latimer was familiar with the area.

While driving, he said, 'The main thing is not to disturb the scene. If it does turn out to be a suspicious death we need to be very careful in what we do because the entire house becomes a murder scene. Our official photographers will arrive soon as well as scenes of crime specialists, and of course, the police doctor. Sergeant Blaketon will have seen to all that.'

The police doctor for Strensford was Dr Tony Easton, who was one of the surgeons working at Strensford District Hospital. Every divisional police station such as Strensford, which had responsibility for a wide rural area along with a few market towns and several villages, was served by a doctor who specialized in police matters. Some police doctors also attended to illnesses and injuries which had occurred on duty among serving officers. Police doctors were professionals who had been trained in the requirements of the police particularly where crime was involved. They were taught the need to preserve evidence, how to cope with fatal or serious traffic or industrial accidents, suicides, sudden deaths, abortions and a host of such matters that formed part of police work. They were, in fact, the precursors of the forensic service which now performs similar duties with modern sophistication.

When we arrived, two marked police cars were parked outside number 19 with uniformed constables in attendance, one of whom was PC Alf Ventress. He stood near the front door to deal with unauthorized visitors trying to enter or peer through the windows. Inevitably a small crowd had assembled in the street and was itself attracting interest from passers-by and people living locally; the easiest way to disperse such 'gawpers', as we called them, was to obtain their names and addresses.

If that didn't move them on, we'd ask what they knew about the incident and tell them we required a written statement from each person. Crowds rapidly thinned in the face of such a threat. A uniformed bobby was already doing that.

I followed DS Latimer to the front door where Alf Ventress was looking important and rather fierce.

'You were first on the scene, I'm told,' began Latimer. 'So what's the story, Alf?'

'I managed to get some useful background from the neighbour, Mrs Wallace, but she is very upset by it all,' Alf began. 'It started when Mrs Wallace came round as usual to see if she and Miss Scott were going shopping in town before having a coffee but she found the kitchen door locked. It's at the back of the house, her usual way in. She thought it was odd because Miss Scott always got up early and unlocked the back door. Mrs Wallace came round to the front door to ring the bell but got no reply so she looked through the kitchen window and saw her friend on the floor. She rushed home to get a key – she keeps a front door key – and went in to tend her friend. She was apparently unconscious on the floor, which was covered with blood that seemed to have oozed from a wound in her neck. Mrs Wallace realized her friend was seriously injured and probably dead, so she called the local doctor.

'We wondered if Miss Scott might have fallen downstairs and banged her head but the doctor reckoned she couldn't have reached the kitchen with such a serious cut, which looked like a stab wound. He realized there was no trail of blood from the stairs to the kitchen. There's nothing in the kitchen she could have banged her head on to cause such an injury, no signs of blood or hair on the edges of the table, sink, fittings and so on. Mrs Wallace pointed out that the kitchen window was standing open so it looked as if someone had broken in and attacked her, but heaven knows why, she's only a poor old pensioner. She'd only have a few pounds in the house, pension money. Not worth killing for but there are vague rumours she was rich with cash hidden somewhere in the house. Apparently it's not the first time she's been raided.'

'There'll be details in our files if that ever happened,' said Latimer. 'So was she fully dressed or in her nightclothes when she was found?'

'In her nightdress,' responded Alf. 'But she was known to get up early. Maybe she heard a noise and came down to confront the intruder?'

'That's likely. Did the doctor give any hint about the time of death?'

'Well, obviously he can't give an accurate time, that will have to wait until the post mortem, but he thought she had lain there for some time because her blood was congealing. He also thought rigor mortis was present but that can begin to disappear after twenty-four hours.'

'So had the kitchen window been smashed to allow entry?' asked Latimer.

'Not smashed, Sarge, but it might have been forced open using a knife or something with a slim blade. The glass wasn't broken but with some careful manoeuvring, the catch could have been opened from the outside. The surrounding woodwork shows no damage though – it's a very professional entry.'

'Professional?' queried Latimer.

'Well, a practised housebreaker perhaps. These older window frames are easy meat for skilled burglars and breakers – there are no tool marks, for example. Once the window was open, it could admit an adult intruder but remember there are no footprints on the interior window ledge or the sink unit, and no evidence of residue on the floor.'

'An inside job, then? Is that what you are suggesting?'

'It's an option,' said Ventress.

'We'll bear that in mind. So has the house been searched yet?' asked Latimer.

'I searched it briefly when I arrived, Sarge, being first on the scene,' said Alf. 'I'm accustomed to this. I deal with most of the town's sudden deaths so I was very careful. I did not disturb any evidence but I wanted to be sure nobody was hiding on the premises, in the bedrooms, loft and so on. Miss Scott was where she is now, lying on the kitchen floor with the window open. The intruder had clearly made good his escape but there's no evidence of his means of exit. Both doors are Yale latches so he could have made his exit through either one. I made no attempt to revive her; I could see it was too late. She's not the first dead body I've had to deal with but most were natural deaths, not murders or suicides.'

'So were there any breakfast pots on the table? Or in the sink awaiting washing up?'

'No, the table and sink were clear. No sign of any breakfast.'

'You've discovered a lot in a short time,' I praised Alf, who'd lost none of his ability to recall such detail.

'I was never any good at passing promotion exams, Nick, but when we were young coppers undergoing our training, we were taught to be observant. Kim's Game and so on. Very instructive. It has helped me down the years to make a lasting mental impression of scenes like this. Very useful when dealing with any sudden death, suspicious or not. You learn a lot in those first few minutes spent quietly at the scene and I find people are willing to talk without me appearing to interrogate them!'

'And that's all to our mutual benefit,' said Latimer. 'Anything else I should know, Alf?'

'There was no one else on the premises but both beds were unmade.'

'Both beds?' queried Latimer.

'Her bedroom was a mess. I thought it had been searched by a burglar with stuff all over the place, floor covered and drawers pulled out. She has a spare room, Sarge, and has taken in a lodger to get a bit more money for her daily needs and his room was also a mess, as if it had been searched. She's often had lodgers. This one's a 19-year-old lad, a trainee reporter with the *Gazette*, but he'd gone to work by the time the alarm was raised. So far as I know, he'll be unaware of this but if the bush telegraph of Strensford gets to work, the *Gazette* will soon know about it and he'll be informed. I don't know his name but I would expect him to come and see all this for himself, both to get a full report for the *Gazette* and to see what's happened to his landlady and check his own belongings. He might have had something stolen from his room. So far, I don't think he's tried to get in touch so he might not yet be aware of what's happened.'

'Unless he's keeping a low profile, Sarge?'

'You think it's an inside job, Alf?'

'That's my instinct, Sarge. I reckon Miss Scott was lying where she is now *before* he went out to work. After attacking her, he trashed the house to make it look like an intruder, opened the kitchen window from the inside to suggest a means of entry and then disappeared off to work as if nothing had happened. With his bedroom being above the kitchen, he must have heard noises. Surely he'd have done something about it, if only to dial 999.'

'That's all speculation, surely?'

'I prefer to say it's based on long experience, Sarge, ably supported by a bit of gut instinct.'

'Right, Alf. All this means we must find him and interview him,' affirmed Latimer. 'He's a clear suspect and might know of any contacts Miss Scott might have had. If he turns up here, I want to talk to him, Alf; if not, I'll seek him out at the newspaper offices. Now, is Sergeant Blaketon here? The office said he'd be here.'

'He's arrived, yes, but decided to visit nearby houses to ask if they heard any suspicious noises during the night, or have seen anyone prowling about.'

'A good idea. I'll catch up with him in due course. Now I need to look around the house; come with me, Nick but be careful where you put your feet and don't touch anything. I need to know as much as possible before Detective Chief Superintendent Marshall and his squad arrive from headquarters. He likes us to get cracking right away to establish the preliminary details and trace any witnesses or even suspects.'

I should add that this incident occurred long before the modern system with its meticulous preservation of crime scenes. In this case, I put my feet down carefully and refrained from touching anything that might bear fingerprints or other evidence as I followed DS Latimer into the small terraced house. He did not speak, beginning upstairs with Miss Scott's dishevelled room.

Next he inspected the lodger's room, which was in a similar state, then the bathroom, upstairs toilet and small loft. Downstairs he went into the small, neat lounge, dining room, downstairs toilet and kitchen, again not speaking but absorbing every detail. Then PC Ventress hailed him from outside the front door.

'Sarge!' he called to Latimer. 'I've got Tim Drummond outside, he wants a word.'

'Drummond?' queried Latimer.

'Miss Scott's lodger, the reporter from the *Gazette*.'

'Right! I'll come out,' said Latimer. 'The interior is sealed off, including Mr Drummond's room. Come along, Nick, I want you to hear this.'

Standing beside Alf Ventress outside the front door was a tall, dark-haired young man dressed in a smart dark blue suit. He would be at least six feet tall, athletic in build whilst presenting himself as clean and smart, apart from a day's growth of beard around his jaw-line.

'Mr Drummond? I'm Detective Sergeant Latimer from the local CID, and this is DC Rhea, a newcomer to our ranks. I'm not sure what you have been told but we are making a preliminary search and preserving the scene in this house because we suspect a crime has been committed. Your landlady, Miss Scott, has been attacked, apparently by an intruder, and is lying in the kitchen.'

'I heard at the *Gazette* … a freelance noticed the activity and filed a report so I came straight here to see if I can do anything. Is she badly hurt?'

'I'm afraid Miss Scott is dead, Mr Drummond. We are treating this as a suspicious death at this early stage.'

'Oh my God … this is dreadful … she is … was … such a kind lady …'

'Was she a relation?' asked Latimer.

'No, not even remotely. I was given her address when I got the job of reporter; she has often taken in new reporters and other staff when they first arrive. Being here gives me time to look for a place of my own.'

'You're not local then?'

'No, I'm from Manchester but I liked the idea of working at the seaside.'

'So, Mr Drummond, forgive me interviewing you out here like this, but right now we have nowhere else ...'

'It's no problem, Sergeant. Please continue, I want to help all I can. Am I allowed to report this in the *Gazette*?'

'You can relate the facts, Mr Drummond, but without speculating on the outcome. There is much to be done before we can be sure of the circumstances. If you are in doubt about what to publish, come and talk to me. Meanwhile, can you tell me about your movements this morning?'

'There's not a lot I can say except that I slept in. It's our early start today as we plan the first proofs of the newspaper, decide on illustrations and fillers if needed, so I skipped breakfast and dashed straight out of the front door. It's quicker than going out of the back door and round by the rear terrace ...'

'So you didn't stop long enough to dash into the kitchen and grab a dish of cornflakes or a cup of tea?'

'No,' said the reporter. 'I came straight downstairs and rushed out of the front door. I can always get a snack at work. I had no time to straighten my bed, get a shave or even explain my urgency to Miss Scott. I never had the time or a reason to go into the kitchen this morning.'

'Not even to call to Miss Scott to say you were off to work?'

'I didn't know she was she in the kitchen, Sergeant. I never heard her.'

'So did you sleep soundly last night? Were you disturbed by any noises, especially in the house? The kitchen in particular. I believe it's directly beneath your room.'

'It is but I slept very well, never heard a thing. As I said, I slept late.'

'It seems the attack took place in the kitchen, Mr Drummond. Directly beneath your room. And Miss Scott's bedroom was ransacked; it's next to yours. I'd have thought all that activity would have woken you. I've reason to believe it all occurred *before* you went to work. I find it hard to believe you weren't aware of something that needed your attention. You say you were late but it would have taken only a couple of seconds to pop your head around the kitchen door to tell Miss Scott you were leaving for work. If you'd done that, you'd have seen her lying on the floor. She always got up early, we're told, so you'd expect her to be in the kitchen, probably preparing breakfast. You might have saved her life, Mr Drummond, stemmed her bleeding or sought help.'

'Look, Sergeant, I really was terribly late …'

'So tell me again. What time did you leave the house?'

'About ten to eight, to be in the office by eight.'

'And were you?'

'Made it by the skin of my teeth!'

'I still can't believe you slept through all that activity. Now can I ask this? Did you come downstairs and go into the kitchen for any reason between, say, bedtime last night and eight this morning?'

'I made myself a cup of cocoa last night about ten o'clock and sat in the lounge to drink it; she'd gone upstairs by then. I rinsed my mug, put it away and went to bed before eleven.'

'Locking up before you went upstairs?'

'Checking doors and windows, yes. The house was secure. She checks all the doors and windows but so do I before I go upstairs. I'm usually last to bed. The house was totally secure, Sergeant. I'd have thought no one could have got in without me knowing but it seems I was wrong.'

'So if I believe your account of things, the intruder must have climbed in through the kitchen window without disturbing you, even though he would have to force it open. You are sure it was properly closed?'

'I've told you it was, I checked. He must have found a way to open it.'

'And without keys, there was no other way in. Both doors were locked.'

'Absolutely. He must have been a skilled burglar to force it open without breaking the glass.'

'So how do you know the glass was not broken if you've not been in the kitchen since ten o'clock last night, making cocoa?'

'I … er …'

'There's more, Mr Drummond. If the intruder had entered that way, there'd be evidence on the interior window sill, kitchen sink, draining board … he'd have to clamber over those surfaces to get in, but there's no evidence he did that, Mr Drummond! In fact, I think the window was opened from the *inside* to give the impression of an intruder.' He paused, continuing a moment later. 'But now it's time to have your fingerprints taken and your clothing examined for bloodstains that may match Miss Scott's blood group, so that means a trip to the police station.'

'You can't suspect me, surely?'

'But I do, Mr Drummond. Now, DC Rhea, I think it's time for your first arrest of a suspected murderer. Got your handcuffs?'

'Special lightweight ones for the CID, Sergeant, here in my trouser pocket.' I withdrew the light aluminium cuffs to approach Drummond. As I did so, I chanted the short caution, the vital element of an arrest. 'You are not obliged to say anything …'

'You've no evidence, not a scrap!' protested Drummond.

I completed the formal wording of the caution as DS Latimer came and seized Drummond's right elbow. 'You are now under arrest, Mr Drummond, but I want you to know that our actions may also establish your innocence. We might clear you of suspicion. For that, we need all your clothes, towels, facecloths and so on, for scientific analysis. We need to prove you were not at the scene at the time of Miss Scott's death, that you did not open the kitchen window from the inside to make it appear as if an intruder had entered, and of course we need to establish your motive. Did she have a secret place to hide her savings? Was money the motive? Are you prepared for us to proceed along those lines? If necessary, we shall search all the refuse deposits in this area, dustbins and so on, looking for cast clothing that might be yours, as well as any other evidence you might have disposed of, such as the murder weapon. A kitchen knife, perhaps, bearing Miss Scott's bloodstains. It does seem as if you had a busy night, Mr Drummond, one that made you almost late for work without even having time for a shave.'

He paused a moment, then turned to me. 'Get a car, Nick, there are some outside with drivers. Get one to take you and your customer to the police station. I'll come too.'

'I'll sue you for all this!' shouted Drummond.

'Good, then you'll have a good story for your editor. If I were you, Mr Drummond, I'd not say a word.'

Faced with the inevitable, Drummond later admitted the murder of Miss Scott; he was deeply in debt. He'd been searching her room for hidden savings said to be somewhere in the house; she'd fled downstairs and he'd caught her in the kitchen, silencing her with a carving knife from a drawer. Then he'd attempted a cover-up, making it look like the work of an intruder.

The murder weapon was recovered by Sergeant Blaketon from a neighbour's dustbin where it had been thrown in the hope it would be carried away by the dustmen. It was Sergeant Blaketon's visits to houses near that of Miss Scott that had led to this particular householder saying he'd been woken by noises around 3 a.m. and had thought it was a scavenging fox investigating his dustbin. He'd forgotten about it until Sergeant Blaketon had knocked on his door. Later analysis proved that bloodstains on the blade corresponded to Miss Scott's blood group.

At the assizes, Tim Drummond pleaded guilty to murder and received a life sentence. Miss Scott indicated in her will that she wanted a wildlife charity to receive £8,000; all her money was safe within a bank with very little kept in the house.

And I had arrested my first murderer!